The Game
of Life

The Game

of Life

Norma Howe

Crown Publishers, Inc.
New York

Published by Crown Publishers, Inc., 225 Park Avenue South, New
York, New York 10003

CROWN is a trademark of Crown Publishers, Inc.
Manufactured in the United States of America

Library of Congress Cataloging-in-Publication Data

Howe, Norma, The game of life / by Norma Howe. Summary: A
young girl learns about growing up when she inadvertently maims her
young cousin.
    [1. Family relations—Fiction.] I. Title.
PZ7.H8376Gam   1989   [Fic]—dc19   88-26899
ISBN 0-517-57197-8

10 9 8 7 6 5 4 3 2 1

First Edition

For the Knotheads—and their mother

The Game
of Life

1

My name is Cairo Hays, and I've lived on a short, curving street called Cloverdale Circle all of my life. I used to think that Cloverdale Circle was just an average American middle-class street, but after getting around and seeing a little more, I'm convinced that it must be higher than so-called middle class. The lawns in my neighborhood are always trimmed, and there are no junk cars in the driveways or lopsided sofas and rusty washing machines strewn around on the porches like on Rocky Nevin's street. But then, even Rocky's neighborhood looks like paradise city if you compare it to the really slummy parts of town south of the river. Until just recently I felt (subconsciously) that if you lived in a better neighborhood, you were automatically a better person. Now, however, mostly because of Rocky, I think I understand that life is a little more complicated than that.

The newest people on Cloverdale Circle (Pete and Linda Rogers) live in the little redbrick house directly across the street from us. The Rogerses always have four or five cats hanging around their place. Every time they open their front door, a few dart in and a few dart out—calicoes, tabbies, alley cats, you name it. That couple seems to go through cats like most people go through light bulbs. I suppose I should be grateful for the Rogerses, though, since they go away for the weekend quite often and ask either my younger sister, Mercedes, or me, to feed the cats and change their litter boxes while they're gone. The boxes are always such a disaster; at first we didn't know what to make of it. But then Mercedes figured out what the Rogerses do. "They *never* clean out the litter," she said. "They just wait until they can't stand it anymore, and then they go away for the weekend and leave the mess for you or me." But they pay well, and lately Mercedes and I have agreed to take turns doing the job, no matter who answers the phone when they call.

Ever since they moved in, Mercedes, who's thirteen, has been going around telling everyone that now we live in Mr. Rogers's neighborhood.

René Bonfiglio has lived on Cloverdale Circle all of her life, too. Actually, her name is René Bunney now, since her stepfather has legally adopted her. (I thought it was odd that her mother would let her change her name, but Mom told me that Mr. and Mrs. Bonfiglio were on the verge of a divorce before he died, so that explained it.) When you've known someone all her life by one name, it's sure hard to get used to calling her something different. René lives two doors away, on the other side of the Goldsmiths' place, and is sixteen, like me. Her real father used to jog five miles every morning in Italian shorts (red, white, and green) and then swim ten laps in their pool, rain or shine, winter and summer. In the winter, that pool must have been freezing. When René was eight years old, Mr. Bonfiglio was electrocuted in a freak accident on the roof of their house. He was trying to fix the TV antenna in a rainstorm so René could watch the Saturday morning cartoons. You'd think she'd feel guilty about that, but she's never said anything about it to me.

I guess that's not so strange when you stop to think about it. I have guilty feelings, too, that I've never told her about. I've never even talked to her about my little cousin Jerry, and I've never repeated to her what his hysterical mother screamed at me so long ago, after she'd seen the terrible thing I had done to his fingers. (Oh, God, won't I *ever* forget about that?)

I met Rocky Nevin in a bingo parlor. The reason I was there was all on account of an article my mom read in the Sunday supplement called "Dealing with Today's Puzzling Teenager." The whole point of the article was—well, let's say your teenager is a slobbo who never cleans their room. (Ms. Andes, my English teacher, says that in her class it is perfectly acceptable to say, "Your *teenager* is a slobbo who never cleans *their* room," even though the noun is singular and the pronoun is plural. Ms. Andes is a feminist and darned proud of it. She says it's better to use *their* than *his, his, his,* all the time.) Anyway, the parent is supposed to say something like, "Darling, let's make a deal. You clean your room, and you can have dinner here on a regular basis."

The deal my mom had in mind was what the article called a "reverse twist." She wanted me to do her a favor, and in return she'd do something special for me. (The article didn't say so, but to me that sounded like an old-fashioned bribe.) The favor she wanted me to do was to accompany her to the bingo parlor, located at the Bel Aire Shopping Mall, every Wednesday night so she wouldn't have to go alone and get raped in the parking lot.

"It's only a couple of hours," she told me. "You could bring your homework."

"But, Mom," I whined, *"every* Wednesday?" I knew I would end up going. I was only trying to fatten up my end of the deal.

But my mother put all her cards on the table in one swell foop.

"Cairo," she said, "I'll probably live to regret this, but here's what I'll do." She took a deep breath. "I'll let you get a puppy."

I had to let that sink in for a second, because I couldn't believe my ears. I have been begging for a puppy ever since I could talk.

"A live one?" I asked slowly.

"Oh, fun*ny,*" she said.

* * *

The same Sunday supplement that had the article about making deals with today's teenager also had another article, one that was of particular interest to me. It was in the form of a little quiz, and it was called "Test Your Honesty." René was over and we were reading the Sunday paper and eating donuts in the dining room, and I suggested we take the test together. Ever since I was a little kid I've worried about whether I'm basically honest or not, so I felt really good when I scored 42 ("very honest") while René got 27 ("borderline"). She got mad and said she didn't think the test had much validity. "You could have been lying when you answered the questions," she said. "What about that?"

"Well, I wasn't," I answered, inwardly offended that she could even suggest such a thing.

We sat there for a few minutes, with me trying to read the comics again, and her still checking out that test. I looked up and saw that she was watching me. "I wasn't," I repeated. "I wasn't lying, René!"

She suddenly turned nasty, the way she does sometimes. "And just who, pray tell, was the one who stole the candy bar from Hart's Drugs that time on the way home from school?" she asked, head tipped sideways and dark eyebrows raised slightly. "A Milky Way, if memory serves."

I was shocked to hear her dredge that up. "René," I said, "we were in the first grade, for God's sake!"

After a minute I glanced up at her again. She was still examining the edge of the newspaper where I had marked my answers, but I was suddenly transported back in time to that wintry November day when I lifted a candy bar from Mr. Hart's display and quickly dropped it into the folds of my yellow umbrella. Mr. Hart followed us out of the store. "Just a minute, girls!" We stopped and turned, and my breath caught in my throat as I saw him standing there, his white smock flapping in the wind. He was pointing at my folded umbrella. "What do you have in there?" "Nothing," I whimpered softly, as he separated the yellow folds and peered down into them. Then he reached in his long arm and pulled out the Milky Way. "Young lady, what is your phone number?" he demanded. That night, when the phone finally rang, I knew it was Mr. Hart. My father spoke with him for what seemed like a hundred years. Finally, Dad quietly hung up the phone and looked at me. "Cairo," he said, "you have two choices. You can either grow up to be a nasty, sniveling little thief who is always in trouble and is a disgrace to your family, or you can vow never to lie, cheat, or steal again. Which will it be?" My sisters and my mother had come into the room by then, and they were all looking at me with big eyes and downcast faces. I didn't know the meaning of the word *sniveling*, but it sounded disgusting. "Oh, Daddy, Daddy," I cried, "the second one, the second one!" And I meant it with all my heart.

"Okay, look at this one!" René said, bringing me back to the present with a jolt. "Question four." She read it. "Would you lie to protect a friend?"

She reached over across the table and tapped my arm. "You checked no on that one," she said, accusingly.

"So?"

René tossed down her pencil stub. "You mean to say, like, if—well, say that some Nazi SS Trooper asked you if I was Jewish, would you say that I wasn't?"

"Well, you're *not*, birdbrain. Jeez!"

"Yeah," she persisted, "but let's say I was. What if I was Jewish and the Nazis asked you if I was, and if I was, it would mean certain death. Would you lie and say I wasn't, or would you let them drag me off to the gas chamber?"

"This is crazy," I said. "You've been watching too many old movies."

"It's not crazy, Cairo!" She hit her fist on the table for emphasis. "I'm not going to sit here and get a reputation for dishonesty when you don't even understand the significance of what we're discussing." She stood up. "I'm going home."

"Oh, sit down, René. Here, have another donut." I took a deep breath and then let it out all at once while I thought about what she had said.

"Okay," I finally admitted. "I guess I *would* lie in a case like that—where the situation itself is unusual and immoral. The same thing like in a bank robbery, for instance. If the robber asked me if I had any jewelry, and I had my poor old grandmother's emerald brooch in my sock, well, sure, I would lie, I guess. I wouldn't have to tell the truth in a case like that. Not to a bank robber, anyway."

René hesitantly reached for another donut and sat down. "Your grandmother's emerald brooch, in your sock?"

We started reading the paper again. But René never knows when to quit. "What if it was *ill-gotten gains?*" she asked suddenly, raising her eyebrows suggestively, like a second-rate police inspector in some old TV rerun.

I looked up, annoyed. Sometimes René's train of thought seems to veer right off the track. "What if *what* was ill-gotten gains? What are you talking about?"

"Your grandmother's emerald brooch, of course! What if your grandmother stole the brooch? What if she *stole* it, see, and it didn't belong to her in the first place? Would that make any difference? Would it be okay to lie to the robber about a *stolen* brooch?"

I put my elbows on the table and rubbed my eyes. "Jeez, René," I breathed.

"I don't think it would," she continued before I could even answer. "If the brooch in your sock was stolen by your grandmother, you'd probably have to tell the truth to the robber, if you want to get really technical about it."

That settled, she picked up the pencil again and chewed the end of it while she started to flip the pages of Macy's advertising supplement.

But I was still thinking about what she had said. Talk about convoluted logic! All the same, I wasn't about to let her get the best of this argument if I could help it. I scored "very honest" in the quiz, and I resented the fact that she was trying to discredit the test somehow. "Okay, René," I began. "What about this? What if my grandmother stole the emerald brooch from the *Nazis?* Huh? Figure that one out."

"Hmm," René mused, taking up the challenge. She stopped sketching mustaches on the Macy's models and stared off into space. "Let's see now. If your grandmother stole the emerald brooch from the Nazis, and you had it in your sock when the bank robber came in . . ."

Mercedes walked into the dining room just then and looked at me with a puzzled expression. She waggled her thumb in René's direction and asked in a bewildered tone, "What is she *talking* about?"

Altogether, there are seventeen people in my extended family. Since one of my grandmothers died five years ago, that leaves my parents (two), my remaining grandparents (three), my sisters (two), my aunts and uncles (six), my cousins (three), and me (one). Two of my cousins (Jerry and Dawn) and their parents (Aunt Ginger and Uncle Walter Spender) are estranged from the family, because of me. They moved to Phoenix about a month after the accident (involving the fingers) and we never even correspond or send greeting cards of any kind. A very eerie thought occurred to me one sleepless night not long after they left: Jerry rhymes with strawberry, and Spender rhymes with blender.

*　　*　　*

My parents like to tell how they learned some-thing incredible about each other on their very first date. Out of the Seven Wonders of the World, they both wanted to see the very same two sometime during their lives. One is the Taj Mahal (in India) and the other is the pyramids at Giza.

They haven't seen the Taj Mahal yet, but they went over to Egypt seventeen years ago to see the pyramids. The only thing they didn't like about the trip was that they couldn't find even one little item to add to their collection of patented kitchen gadgets—affectionately known in our family as "PKG's" (Patented Kitchen Gadgets). They hunt for them everywhere—thrift stores, garage sales, flea markets—all those kinds of places. The fact is, they met twenty-two years ago in the kitchenwares department at a St. Vincent De Paul Thrift Store near Everett, Washington, where they used to live. They said it was funny, because the store had somehow gotten hold of a bunch of those stick-on name tags that people wear at conventions—the kind that say, HI! MY NAME IS ＿＿＿＿, and a clerk at the store had the brilliant idea of using those name tags to label the various bins in which they kept their small used merchandise. My mother said she was going around the store reading name tags that said, HI! MY NAME IS Pots and Pans, and HI! MY NAME IS Children's Underwear, and HI! MY NAME IS Belts and Wallets. She and my dad met and fell in love at the HI! MY NAME IS Kitchen Gadgets bin and have been collectors ever since. "Old Number One" is a patented left-handed eggbeater for which they paid fifteen cents ("a steal"). They keep it on top of the fireplace mantle, right alongside pictures of the pyramids and the Taj Mahal. I used to think my parents were slightly crazy because of their collection of PKG's, but then our local newspaper sponsored a "Bizarre Collection Contest," which really opened my eyes. The winner was this guy who collected advertising flyswatters (PACKAGING PROBLEMS? CALL YOUR LANDSBERG SWAT TEAM). The runner-up collected dirty old run-over socks that she found on streets and highways. She said it was surprising how many of them you could find out there.

Even though my parents didn't come home from Egypt with any kitchen gadgets, they made up for it with color slides. They must have about two million of them (35mm) that they took while they were on that trip. They also have a couple of dozen stories—little incidents that happened while they were over there—that we all know by heart. They like to brag about what cheap little fleabag places they stayed at and how lunch usually cost them the equivalent of thirty-five cents in American money. Now whenever they get a dirty spoon in a restaurant or there's a hair in their sandwich or something, one of them says with a little self-mocking smile, "Oh, that's okay. We've been to Egypt."

Once my mom cut open a loaf of French bread and sliced off the head and front section of a huge black cricket that was baked inside. She stood there at the breadboard, immobilized, just staring at the crumpled legs and making a sound like "*Achhh*" from somewhere deep in her throat.

"Hey, that's okay, Mom," Mercedes said, playfully putting her arm around Mom's shoulder and patting her back. "Heck, you've been to *Egypt*."

I don't know why that was so funny, but it was, especially when it took my mom a couple of seconds to catch on. She still had that shocked expression on her face, and she turned to look at Mercedes and said weakly, "What, dear? What did you say?" And then it dawned on her. She put her hand to her forehead and collapsed in a chair, bent over with laughter.

My older sister, Heather, was about two years old when my folks went on that trip (they left her with my grandparents), and Mom found out she was pregnant with me when they got home. At first they only joked back and forth about naming me Cairo, but when the time came, they just went ahead and did it.

Cairo, full of mystery and intrigue, is also known as a city of contrasts: rich and poor, old and new, sun and shadows, and laughter and tears. So Cairo is a good name for me, I think. And Cairo Hays is even better. One of my parents' slides from Egypt was taken just at sunset from the top of a famous tower in the middle of Cairo, and you can see that the city is crowned by a hazy golden mist. My dad said it's a combination of moisture from the Nile and the wind-borne sand that engulfs the area. (Cairo *Hays*, indeed.) I've often wondered if I would have become a different person (more ordinary?) if I had been given a name like Linda or Debbie. As it is, I've always thought of myself as a unique kind of oddball, just a little out of step with the world. Cairo Hays, that's me.

Two years after I was born, Mom got pregnant for the last time. It was another little girl, and they named this one Mercedes, since Dad said he figured that was the only way he'd ever get one. Can you believe it—naming a kid just so he could make a joke about a car?

Every Fourth of July we have a big block party on Cloverdale Circle. Each family on the street is supposed to bring a complete meal—like salads and hot dogs and dessert and watermelon. When it's time to eat, we put all the food out and everybody in the neighborhood just wanders around and takes what they want, and we all end up sitting on our neighbor's lawn and eating each other's food. It's really lots of fun, and we're even famous, since three years ago a photographer from the newspaper came out and took a picture, and the Cloverdale Circle Fourth of July Block Party was featured on the Metro page the next day.

Anyway, around the last week in June, my mother lists the names of all our family members who live in town and calls them up to see what they want to bring. My mother's only brother, Uncle Larry, always wants to bring the potato chips. It's gotten to be kind of joke. "Uncle Larry will bring the potato chips," we always say, and then we laugh. Larry is forty-six years old, is very rich, and has never been married. Grandpa Bottoms (Mom, Aunt Ginger, and Uncle Larry's father) is really getting fidgety about the "never married" part, since Larry happens to be the last living male in the Bottoms family, and unless he marries and has a son, the family name will die out. (Or, as Mercedes said, "The Bottoms will drop out.") It's the old macho thing about leaving your mark on the world. The way Grandpa B figures, daughters don't seem to count, only sons. My mom thinks that whole idea is stupid, and of course my sisters and I agree. "You've *got* grandchildren, Dad," she said to him once, barely moving her lips. "Where?" he said, acting dumb and looking all around. And then he winked at me, but I didn't think he was funny at all.

My father's full name is Edward Raymond Hays. He has two sisters (one married and one divorced), and some people in the family have been trying to match up rich Uncle Larry (my mother's brother) with my father's thirty-five-year-old divorced sister, Lucille. She weighs 207 pounds (I saw the scale) and laughs a lot with a full, musical, joyous sound, but none of us think she's really happy. That laugh is just a cover-up. Her marriage was broken up by her former mother-in-law. The "old bag," as Lucille calls her, never did like her, and even called her a "big fat slob" right to her face. The old lady badgered her constantly, and Lucille's spineless husband just sat there and refused to take sides. We don't know how she stood it, but Lucille hung in there for five years (and two miscarriages) before finally deciding to call it quits. Soon after the divorce, her former husband married the slender girl his mother had picked out for him all along. Her name was Miss Belinda Madrigal, and she worked at the donut shop where we always used to go for our Sunday morning donuts. (Naturally, after all of that, we switched to Winchell's in deference to Aunt Lucille's feelings.) I think that Belinda Madrigal is one of the most beautiful sounding names I have ever heard, but of course I've never told that to Aunt Lucille.

My suspicions about Aunt Lucille's wonderful laugh being just a cover-up for her unhappiness were confirmed when she recently confided in me about a recurring nightmare she's been having for months. (I wanted to tell the others in my family, since they suspect the same, but I promised Lucille I wouldn't.) Anyway, she said she just had to tell someone, so she picked me. In this dream, she's always seated at a huge banquet table with lots of elegantly dressed people and loads of food. Everyone else is stuffing themselves with mashed potatoes and gravy (her favorites), gooey chocolate sundaes, and avocado sandwiches, and yet they are becoming skinnier and skinnier, while she is not eating a mouthful, yet keeps getting fatter and fatter, until she finally explodes.

I tried to sympathize with her and comfort her as best I could. We were sitting out on the front steps at the time, and after she told about the dream, she just looked at me hopelessly as if to say, "Well, pretty awful, isn't it?"

I instinctively reached over and grabbed her arm and pressed my head up against it for a minute. That's when she turned away from me and whispered, "God, Cairo, I hate being so fat and ugly."

It was the first time I ever heard her say anything like that. And it really bothered me. All this time—all my life, in fact—I had just thought of her as good old fat Aunt Lucille.

"Gee," I muttered, "I don't know what to say. I mean, you're such a neat person, Lucille. You've got this great personality, and you're not ugly! I just never even think about how you look. Really I don't."

She shifted her weight around on the cement step and acknowledged my comments with a disbelieving grunt. "So you never think about how I look, huh? That's funny, because I hardly think about anything else."

One of the Rogerses' cats bounded across the street just then and came over to join our conversation. "This is Affirmative Action," I said, reaching down to pet him. "The Rogerses seem to have a lot of fun naming all their cats," I added sarcastically, "but they really don't take very good care of them." (I was hoping I could change the subject.) "See, here's the joke: Notice Affirmative Action is all white, and a neutered male?" I gave her a sick smile. "Get it?"

But Lucille wasn't ready to change the subject

yet. She started to talk about her dream again, going over the details once more. "I was wearing that two-piece lavender outfit I got for my dad's retirement party . . ." Her voice drifted off and she covered her face with her hands.

"I think I know why you dreamed that," I said finally. "It's because of that video we rented—I forget the name—that Monty Python one where the fat guy, you know, in the fancy restaurant, throws up all over the place. Remember, when he eats that gigantic dinner and then the waiter urges him to finish off with that one tiny little thin mint wafer?"

"Oh, God, yeah! I remember that. It was so disgusting."

"Well, I think maybe that's where your brain got the idea. But instead of throwing up, see, you just explode."

She nodded. "I bet you're right," she agreed. "It was that stupid movie. Gosh, that fat man was so gross."

"He's probably a really nice person, though," I added, feeling I should say something complimentary about the poor guy. "Too bad they can't split people like that up into twos or threes . . ."

"Yeah," she said ruefully. "Two of him, two of me. Maybe we could meet, right after the operation, in the splitting recovery room."

"Hey, you all could have a double wedding!" I said brightly, picking up on her morbidly droll mood. But obviously, I went too far. She started laughing at first, not her usual laugh of practiced

17

gaiety, but more of an honest laugh, a short burst, followed immediately by hysterical tears.

"Oh, Lucille!" I exclaimed, leaning over and trying to hug her with both arms. "Oh, I'm sorry! Please! Please don't do that!"

She shook her head, her tears wetting my hand, and suddenly she was laughing again. "Cairo," she said between gasps and tears, "oh, Cairo, you're like a ray of sunshine in my life. Stand by me, honey. Will you stand by me?"

I felt so depressed and helpless. I just wished there was some way I really could help her.

"Hey," I said. "Isn't this half-price day at the Couch Potato? Let's go rent that new Woody Allen movie. Pete Rogers just paid me ten bucks, so it's my treat."

2

My older sister, Heather, who's a sophomore at UC Berkeley, called from there and knocked us all for a loop. She said Allan had just proposed to her, and they were thinking they might want to get married this summer at our Fourth of July block party. She said she and Allan think it would be cute to get married on Independence Day, although they couldn't set the date for sure until Dr. Gabriel, their personal astrologer (and the author of the daily "Stargazing with Gabe" column in the *Berkeley Bugle*) revealed to them their "lucky days" for July.

None of us has even met this Allan guy. All we know about him is what Heather has told us on two previous phone calls, which isn't much. His name is Allan Allen (or maybe Allen Allan—I'm not sure of the spelling) and he's a terrifically handsome thirty-year-old environmentalist who writes country and western tunes and hopes to make it big some day in the entertainment business. Also, he's a Leo. That's very important to Heather.

Heather will be twenty in June. She's a Gemini, with Scorpio rising. (She confided to me once that she can't help it if she's so liberated, sexually. She said it's all Scorpio's doing.) I was in the kitchen with Mom when we got the call announcing their "exciting news." They were phoning from the huge old house called Frogpond, where Allan lives with about a dozen other people. Heather says they're an "interesting mixture." Besides Allan, there are two brothers from Taiwan who work in a Chinese fast-food restaurant, a deaf girl who handcrafts leather purses, a Scientologist recruiter, a guy who owns a pickup truck and does hauling, several dropouts who work at various odd jobs, four undergraduates, three cats, and a parrot. Since Allan was on the extension, my mother felt a bit constrained about telling Heather what she really thought (she told me later), which was that for Heather to get married to a thirty-year-old environmentalist song-writer when she had barely started her own education was about the dumbest thing she ever heard of, even from Heather.

"Does, ah, does this Allan have a job, dear?" was what Mom asked after she had picked herself up from the floor (so to speak). "Oh, I see. He wants *you* to quit school and get a job, does he? He's on the line? Oh, hi there, Allan. Well, I should say! It's nice to meet you, too!" Nervous laugh. "Uh, I was just asking Heather, ah, well, never mind. Here, Heather, talk to Cairo." And then Mom handed the receiver to me and rolled her eyes toward the ceiling, whispering, "Heather's going to quit school and they're talking about getting married on the Fourth of July!"

I grabbed the phone. "Hello," I said. "Heather?"

"Oh, Cairo," she gushed, "it's all perfect! I met him on a day that Dr. Gabriel had predicted would be a real red-letter one for me."

"You told me that last time, Heather," I reminded her. But I guess she didn't hear me.

"Dr. Gabe said I'd meet someone who would have a supreme influence on my life. And there he was, ahead of me in the line at the Seven-Eleven, and sixteen cents short! God, he had this *magnetism*. I knew he was a Leo the minute I laid eyes on him. I knew he *had* to be a Leo, or maybe a Libra, or a Gemini, like me. Hey, Allan"—she laughed, her voice fading, as if she were turning her head and speaking directly to him—"you still owe me that sixteen cents, you big goon."

"Heather?" I said into the phone. "Hey, Heather?" But all I could hear was muffled giggles and scuffling sounds and the telephone bouncing on the floor. Finally Heather came back on the line, but it sounded like she had her hand over the mouthpiece. "Now *stop it*, Allan! I mean it!" She removed her hand. "Cairo? Are you still there? Hello? Hello?"

"Yes, I'm here," I replied. "Listen, Heather, are you guys officially engaged, or what? You've only been going with this one for a month or two, haven't you? Did he give you a ring? And did you tell Mom you were going to *quit school* and get a job? Well, what about your art degree? Remember how you said you wanted to get that great job with the ad agency, and they told you to get your degree and then go back and talk with them? You know, you'd really better think about it some more, Heather. And wait a minute. What about Arthur? I thought you just told me recently that you were thinking about dating Arthur again. You'd better not rush into—"

"Whoa, horse, whoa!" Heather laughed, recalling an old game we used to play when we were little. "Questions, questions! I know what I'm doing, worrywart! Okay!" she hollered suddenly, almost shattering my eardrum. "Listen, Cairo, I've got to hang up now. They're calling me. We're all going out for pizza and beer to celebrate. I'll talk to you later."

She hung up the phone and I slumped down in my chair. Mom was leaning up against the refrigerator and biting her lip. "God, what a flutterhead," I said softly. "What's wrong with her, anyway? I thought she was finally starting to settle down, and now this!"

Heather means well, but she has always been a little spacey, to put it mildly. She's not dumb; I don't mean to say that. After all, she *does* go to Berkeley. And she draws better than anyone I've ever seen. But she's just—well, I think it might have something to do with that "right brain, left brain" stuff. I've often thought that if we could only put Heather and Mercedes in the same stew pot and mix them up good, we'd come up with two more-or-less normal personalities. As it is, one is all right brain and the other is all left. Heather is the ethereal type, full of vibes and hunches, while Mercedes is hard facts and science, through and through. As far as my own brain balance goes, I hope it's correct to say (ahem!) that I don't lean too heavily toward one side or the other.

One thing about Heather—and it's so typical— is that she's a true astrology nut. For a while, when I was younger, she had me into it, too. She started reading my horoscope (Aquarius) to me when I was in kindergarten. Every morning before school she'd first read her own, and then she'd say to me, "Listen up, Cairo, here's yours." By the time I was in the second grade I was sounding out the words myself, with her leaning over my shoulder, prompting. I was fascinated with the whole thing. One day I was warned to *take special care while traveling*," and I fell off my bike. Another time my horoscope said, *"Some good news may come in the mail*," and I got a birthday card from Aunt Lucille with a five-dollar bill enclosed.

And then came that awful, fateful day when I was ten: "*You really shine in the kitchen today, Waterbaby!*" my forecast said. "*A culinary concoction could astound them all, so go ahead and mix it up!*" I had to look up *culinary* and *concoction* in the dictionary, but I understood the rest of it okay.

I met Rocky Nevin on the first Wednesday night I went with my mom to play bingo. He was working in the little snack bar they have there in the Bel Aire Shopping Mall. It's called the Snack Shack, and Rocky's mother is the manager. After my mom found a seat and the bingo game got under way, I went over to the Snack Shack booth to get myself a drink. Rocky was behind the counter reading a paperback book and highlighting it with a yellow marking pen.

"So *you're* the guy who does that to all the books," I said.

He looked up. "Huh?"

I pulled some change out of my pocket. "Oh, never mind. I'd like a small root beer, please."

"Sorry, we don't have small drinks."

"You don't? Well, what do you have?"

He pointed to the menu up on the board behind him. It was that semi-homemade kind with movable letters. Under the heading

DRINKS

(in blue letters) was spelled out

LARGE   X-LARGE   HUMONGOUS

(in red letters).

I looked back at Rocky. His hair, eyebrows, and eyes were the same color, a kind of amber brown with flecks of gold. He was standing behind a high counter, just the right height for him to lean his elbow on while resting his chin in his hand. Only now, instead of resting his chin in his hand, he was covering his mouth with the spread of his thumb and index finger and idly scratching the sides of his face at the same time. By the way his eyes were crinkled at the corners, I knew he was hiding a smile.

"Okay then, let's see your large," I said.

He turned around and whisked a Styrofoam cup off of a foot-high stack. He held it up and turned it around slowly so that I might inspect it.

"That's not large," I said. "That's small."

"Nope," he said. "That's large."

"Oh, I think I get it," I said after a moment. "Around here, small is large."

He sighed and shook his head. "Uh-uh. We don't *have* small, remember?"

"So what's the X-large?" I asked.

He whisked a medium-sized Styrofoam cup off another stack.

"That's not X-large," I said. "That's only regular."

He shook his head again and shrugged. He was wearing a short-sleeved, wraparound white apron, and I noticed that the hair on his arms matched his eyes and eyebrows and the hair on his head. Talk about color coordinated!

"Oh, it's X-large, all right," he said, nodding confidently. "I mean, I should know. I work here, don't I?"

"And the humongous?" I asked. "Let's see the humongous."

He produced a third cup with a flourish.

"Hmm," I said. "Okay then, in that case I guess I'll have a *large* root beer." I said the word *large* in a mocking tone of voice.

He hesitated. "You mean you want the small one?"

"Aha!" I exclaimed, pointing my finger at him, even though I knew he had said it just to be funny.

I could hardly wait for Wednesday night to come around again. But of course it did, and after Mom got settled at her table, I went up to the Snack Shack counter to get my drink. I found out his name was Rocky, because that night he had a plastic name tag pinned on his wraparound apron.

"One *large* root beer?" he asked, smiling and putting down his book. I was thrilled and flattered to see that he remembered me.

The book was the same one he was reading the week before, and when he put it down to get my drink, I saw the name of it. It was called *Let's Go Europe.*

A minor miracle happened: René got a date for our Senior Ball. When that information gets on the grapevine, every junior girl at Lincoln High will tear her hair and cross the name of Jeffrey S. Smith off her computerized list of available escorts. And our Senior Ball is still a year away! It's just crazy how panic and trepidation have already crept into the hearts of us all. But I've finally figured out who's to blame for all this madness: Blaine's Professional Photography Studio, that's who.

Blaine's Professional Photography Studio sends

a team of crack photographers to the Senior Ball each year to set up (in an alcove) a scene complete with Grecian urns and potted palms. Here, the appropriately costumed participants (he in his tux and she in her formal gown) are photographed together in living color, proof for generations to come that they were active and happy members of the Class of 19____. No matter what you did in high school, if you don't graduate with that five-by-seven-inch colored glossy neatly tucked away in your box of memories, you may as well forget it.

So that's something else I've got to start worrying about. I don't care about the stupid dance, but I sure need that picture. I have to prepare for that inevitable day when my future children ask to see it. I certainly wouldn't want them to think their mother was a social misfit who couldn't get a date for the Senior Ball, even though that would be the sad, unvarnished truth.

The day finally came when I could get my puppy. It was too much to hope that Mom would let me keep a dog in the house, so I had to wait until my father could repair some broken places in our backyard fence. It was several weeks before he got around to it, but as soon as it was finished, I called up Aunt Lucille and asked if she would take me over to the Humane Society Animal Shelter on Saturday so I could pick out my puppy. Mercedes came along, too. Mercedes says she likes cats better than dogs, but that dogs are okay.

They had lots of cute puppies there, but the dog

I noticed was a beautiful golden brown full-grown one lying in a cage by the door. A nice girl in a smock was taking us around and showing the different puppies to us and telling us what breeds she thought they were. As she passed the cage by the door, she put her fingers through the wire and let the brown dog lick them. "Poor baby," she crooned. "Poor baby."

"What's wrong with him?" I asked, kneeling beside her and sticking my fingers in the cage, too.

"Oh, nothing," she said, "except that this is his last day. If no one takes him, we've got to put him to sleep tomorrow."

Mercedes was shocked. "How come?" she asked.

"Well, we can only keep them for five days, and everyone wants puppies, you know." She sounded cross.

The brown dog's eyes met mine. It slowly drew itself up to a standing position, still keeping its eyes on me. It was pressing up against the sides of the cage, and some of its hair was pushed through the wire mesh. I ran my hand along the outside of the cage, and as soon as I touched his silky fur, I knew I had found my dog.

"That is the one I want," I said. "I'll take this one."

The girl flipped open the metal latch. "I knew you would." She smiled.

"Look!" Mercedes laughed. "Look at that old tail wag!"

When we got home I named him Bribe, in honor of my mom.

*   *   *

I went to the flea market with my parents on Sunday. On the way over we drove through Cedar Grove Heights, which is quite a ritzy section of town. The lawns in front of those houses look like golf courses, and there are only about four houses to a block since the lots are so large. The homes are really beautiful, especially my favorite, which is a two-story brick colonial with six huge white columns supporting the wide porch. As we approached it, a middle-aged man with a slight paunch and a worried expression came out through the front door and walked hurriedly toward the metallic blue Cadillac parked in the circular drive. A second later a well-dressed woman followed him out and slammed the front door behind her. My dad remarked that the car cost at least thirty thousand dollars, and that those people probably paid more in property taxes than his total yearly wages.

My parents had a good day at the flea market, finding two PKG's that they didn't think they had yet. One was a peculiar sort of potato peeler (I think) and the other was a gadget for separating the yolks from the whites of eggs. They were quite excited over that because it was made out of something called Bakelite, which is an early-type plastic. They paid seventy-five cents for the potato peeler ("highway robbery") but only a dime for the egg separator ("a giveaway").

While they were checking out the potato peeler, I was watching the lady at the next table. She had some old cracked dishes for sale, also some plastic cups, an old pot or two and some partially used spools of thread that were all tangled together in a shoe box. After bickering with another lady for about ten minutes over the price of a partially used-up spool of pink thread, they finally settled on ten cents. The woman who sold the thread walked to where her car was parked in back of her table, reached through the open window and deposited the quarter in a small box that was sitting on the dashboard. Her car was about twenty years old and was covered with dents and bashes. I think it was probably red at one time, but now it was impossible to say for certain.

After we got home, I started thinking about the house in Cedar Grove Heights and the people in the Cadillac, and the lady selling a spool of pink thread for a dime, and I wondered how it could happen that people's lives could be so different. What unlikely series of events occurred, I wonder, that could put some people in a half-million dollar house, and others selling a used spool of pink thread at a flea market for ten cents.

There was a cute "Far Side" cartoon a couple of years ago that I've never forgotten. It showed a dog looking out the car window and calling out to a friend (dog). He had a real smug expression on his face and was saying something like, "Ha ha! I get to go to the store, and then I'm going to the vet's to get tutored!"

Well, when I got Bribe, I found out that I had to agree to get him neutered within thirty days. In order to make sure that I would do it, the girl told me their policy was that I had to leave a deposit with them, which I could get back after the deed was done. When I told Mom that I had to take him to the vet's for an operation and asked if she would drive me over there, we had a little argument about who was going to pay for it. Since Bribe is a male, she didn't think the surgery was really necessary. "And this is merely the beginning," she said, not even giving me a chance to talk. "You wait and see! First it's getting fixed, and then he's definitely going to need heartworm pills. Did you read that article in the paper that said heartworm disease is in our area now? It's just going to be one thing after another."

So naturally I had to remind her that *she* was the one who said I could get a dog in the first place, and didn't she remember where I was spending my Wednesday evenings lately. (Did I feel guilty saying that!) And then I told her that getting him "fixed," as she put it, wasn't *my* idea—it was the Humane Society's *rule*. Apparently that did the trick, because she just sighed and put her checkbook in her purse. Later, during the ride to the vet's, she complained the whole time about all the dog hair Bribe was spreading around in the car.

She was right about the heartworm pills. The vet definitely recommended that Bribe take them. As a precaution, she had to give him a test to make sure he didn't have the disease already (he didn't, thank God), and then the pills themselves cost over ten dollars just for the first bottle.

"That settles it," Mom said grimly, writing out the check. "You're just going to have to start looking for a summer job, Cairo. This is more than I bargained for."

Because of his surgery, we had to leave Bribe at the vet's overnight. The next day, Grandpa B happened to be over, and rather than listen to Mom complain about my dog again, I asked Grandpa B if he could give me a ride to pick him up. So on the way home, Bribe and I sat in the back of my grandfather's Toyota truck, with the end of his leash firmly hooked around my arm. He looked so beautiful with the wind blowing his ears back that it made me happy just to be alive. When we got home, Grandpa B remarked that he looked like part golden retriever to him. He said he bet that dog could swim like a fish. He said we should take him to the river sometime and watch him do his stuff.

I got a fat envelope in the mail. It was an engraved name tag for Bribe that I had recently sent away for. I have the Rogerses to thank for it, in a way. What happened was that it was my turn to feed the cats a couple of weekends ago, and when I went over there, I found a note the Rogerses had left for me, saying that they were sorry but they had run out of cat food. (They had been feeding the poor things just shredded wheat for a week!) They also said they had a new kitten (named Scrambled Eggs) to "replace" Buon Giorno, who had recently been run over. While I was there, I heard some loud mewing from the garage and went out to find

El Rancho Grande was trapped in there again. People who treat their animals like that sure make me sick. I was pretty upset with the Rogerses, because I had some homework to do and I still had to wash my gym clothes, so I didn't have all that time to go running off to the store. I crumpled up their stupid note, and that's when I got the idea that the *real* reason they get new cats all the time is just because they want to show off giving them cutesy names. I thought maybe I should suggest to them that they could do the same thing with goldfish. (Later, when I told that to Mercedes, she just raised her eyebrows in this funny kidding way she has, and said, "Oh, yeah?" and reminded me that our *own* parents weren't doing so badly in the cutesy name department. It took me a minute before I realized she was talking about *us*—me, named for a city, and her, for a car! But then I laughed and said, "Well, at least they don't run out of food and feed us only shredded wheat for a week and accidentally lock us up in the garage all the time!")

Anyway, I walked to the store for the cat food, and while I was in line, this lady with two little kids hanging halfway out of the basket by their ankles asked me if I would mind very much if she went ahead of me, since she had to go pick up a prescription for some cough syrup, and then get some gas, and then get the empty egg cartons from her sister and drop them off at her older kid's nursery school, and blah, blah, blah, so I just let her go ahead of me.

While I was waiting for her to check out, I happened to thumb through the new *Woman's Day*, and I saw a Milkbone Company advertisement where you could send away for this engraved metal name tag (in the shape of a dog biscuit) for your pooch. I took down the address and sent away for it as soon as I got home, and now it was here! It's got Bribe's name, my name, our address, and our phone number on it. I went right out and attached it to his collar.

I saw a TV program ("Nova") that helped me to understand a little better Grandpa B's attitude toward leaving his mark. Apparently, new research has shed light on why some bees and ants are willing to give their lives for the good of the hive (or the hill). That phenomenon had been puzzling to scientists because altruism is not one of your more common traits in nature. The new research shows that the reason these little insects are willing to die for the others is that they all share the same genes. The ants and bees in a particular colony are all sisters. If, by dying, they help ensure the survival of their particular hive or hill, what they're really doing is perpetuating their own genes in an indirect way.

So Grandpa B's problem is that he's just ignorant. He's hung up on the family name, not realizing that his genes have been passed on, and he's already left his mark.

Sometimes it's hard for me to realize that I'm actually descended from Grandpa B. I even asked my mom once when I was little if he really *was* my grandfather, and she just laughed and said, "Oh, yes, he's your grandfather all right!" He's one of those short, wiry-type guys—the kind who always has a cigarette dangling from his lips. And his grammar! God, it's really *atrocious*. Ms. Andes would have a fit if she heard him. Sometimes I get the feeling that he knows better, but he just likes to be obstinate and talk any way he "damn well pleases." He goes around bragging that even though he dropped out of school in the eighth grade, he's made more money than a "truckload of them fancy talkers."

About leaving a mark—well, I guess most everyone wants to leave a mark. I know I do, but not just by having kids. That's too easy. Joyce Hawkins, a girl in my gym class at school, has just made that mark, and I wouldn't say she's that swift. What I'd really like to do is know I made a difference, somehow, in the lives of others or in the world.

To my mind, probably the only redeeming quality about Grandpa B is that he's an animal lover, like me—and *unlike* my mother, who had animals around the house all the time while she was growing up, but can't stand them. She's allergic to cats, and thinks that dogs dig in gardens for the sole purpose of annoying her. Whenever she goes for a walk through the park, she always carries a big stick on account of the dogs. She keeps it handy by the step on the front porch. I can't understand that at all. If I see a stray dog, I'll just get down on one knee and say softly, "Here, boy, come here, pooch," instead of hitting it with a stick. They always come up to me with their tails wagging, and

I give them a pet and maybe a hug, and I ruffle up the hair around their ears and look deep into their eyes. Whenever I do that—look deep into the eyes of an animal—a strange, almost mystical feeling washes over me. It's like I'm somehow (but not really) communing with the unseen force that holds and unites the entire universe. I told that to my sisters once, and their reactions were entirely opposite from each other. Old Heather perked up at once, and said something about the inexplicable reality of animal-human ESP and its linkage with the infinite oneness of the cosmos. But Mercedes just looked askance at her and said she never heard such gibberish. Mercedes is far too practical a person for mystical feelings about communing with the oneness of the cosmos through the eyes of a Yorkshire terrior, no matter how intelligent he is.

One thing that really upsets me (but doesn't bother Grandpa B) is seeing loose dogs in pickup trucks. Even though it's against our state law, some people still do it. The drivers are usually big dopey-looking guys who wear cowboy hats and have bumper stickers that say I ♥ MY MACHINE GUN. One time I was riding in Grandpa B's truck with him and Mom, and one of those jerks pulled up alongside of us at a stoplight. I yelled over to him, "Hey, your dog can fall out of there, you know!" But the big idiot didn't even seem to care. And to show his gratefulness for my helpful suggestion, the guy gave me the finger. Grandpa B wasn't much better. He said I didn't know what I was talking about. "Hell," he said, spitting out the window, "them dogs can take damn good care of themselves. They've got a special kind of balance that humans don't know nothing about."

We had elections at school. René hung around while the Student Council counted the ballots. She finally called me about ten-thirty at night. I had already gone to bed but I wasn't asleep yet.

"Hey, Cairo," she said, "Guess who won it for Junior Varsity Cheerleader."

"Listen, René, I was already in bed."

"Oh, sorry. It was Teresa."

"No kidding."

"Well, see you tomorrow. Sorry if I woke you up."

"You didn't wake me up. Who got it for president?"

"Ted LaHarve, of course."

She ran down the list of other winners and then we said good night and I went back to bed and thought about Teresa Jenner. She transferred into our school when we were in the seventh grade, and René and Nancy Reese (another friend of mine) and I talked about it and decided to become friends with her. We all liked her a lot. She laughed all the time and was a real physical person in a friendly and natural kind of way. We got her on our soccer team and all of a sudden we started winning every game. The only problem with her was she didn't use underarm deodorant, and none of us wanted to hurt her feelings and tell her she needed to. I finally figured out how to do it. I made up this phony club and said we were going to call ourselves The Four Musketeers (René and Nancy were in on it.) Then I drew up the bylaws and stuff, and under the heading "Keeping Fit," I listed things like (1) try to exercise at least ten minutes every day, (2) drink plenty of water, (3) use underarm deodorant daily, (4) get enough sleep. I don't know if Teresa ever saw through my little ruse, but it accomplished its purpose. Nancy Reese moved away the next year, and around the ninth grade Teresa started running around with a party crowd. Now she's Junior Varsity Cheerleader, and the Four Musketeers are only a memory.

I still see Teresa at school, of course. In fact, I just recently went to a party at her house. There was a whole bunch of shouting and running in and out, and kids smoking God knows what and a lot of groping around. This boy Jeffrey (whom I had always thought was just a super guy) was there, and he turned out to be a real jerk. Some of the kids had a big argument and people started swearing and taking sides and Laura Saunders cut her hand real bad on a broken bottle. Raymond Bell and Valerie Grossman had a fight and broke up, and Valerie spent the rest of the evening crying.

I thought about that party for a long time after I got home. What I finally decided was, *Hey, I don't need this! I'm through going to parties for a while.*

I told René, and she said she thinks that will take a lot of guts. In a way I guess she's right, but there may be some cowardice mixed in there, too. I can't figure out if I'm being mature for my age, or regressing back to some more secure but juvenile stage.

The word got around at school that I hate parties, and I enjoyed a brief flurry of attention. Kids I've known for years started coming up to me and asking how come I hated parties all of a sudden. I got kind of carried away. "They're just stupid, that's all," I said. A couple of kids agreed with me, but the more fun-loving types half-smiled at each other and then shrugged and went about their business.

We got a short letter from Heather. It turns out Allan does have a job after all. He's a professional(!) house sitter. Heather wrote that there are scads of people all the way down from the East Bay to San Jose who wouldn't even dream of scheduling their vacations until they make sure Allan's available to sit their house.

Heather included in her letter part of the lyrics from his latest song. They are hoping this may be the one that catches on in a big way. It's called "My Mean Little Angel-Girl Clown."

> *When the bright lights are dimmed*
> *In this honky-tonk town,*
> *And the dry desert wind starts to blow,*
> *I'll miss you my mean little angel-girl clown*
> *'Cause luvin' you's a tough row to hoe.*
>
> *(Chorus)*
> *Luvin' you's a tough row to hoe*
> *Luvin' you's a hard line to tow*

But I'll smile then I'll frown
You won't let me down
My mean little angel-girl clown.

It's not finished yet because, Heather wrote, Allan only composes his music when Dr. Gabriel ("Stargazing with Gabe") tells him he's going through a creative phase. Heather also added that you really had to hear it to appreciate its full effect. She said it has a real haunting quality, especially the way Allan sings it with a special little tremor in his voice.

Mercedes won third place in the eighth-grade Science Follies with her exhibit called "The Hoax of Biorhythms." I was really proud of her, but she was feeling down in the dumps because she didn't get first place. She told me that all she wants from her teenage years is to win first place in the Science Follies. Mercedes has an IQ of about 250 and is wise beyond her years. We talked about Heather's letter, and Mercedes said the more she hears about Allan, the more she thinks he sounds like a genuine weirdo, and a very poor risk, marriagewise. I'm afraid I agree with her, but I don't know what I can do about it, or even if it's my place to try.

The Snack Shack at the bingo parlor closes about eight-thirty, right after the intermission in the bingo game. The third Wednesday I was there, after it closed, Rocky walked over to the table where I was sitting and asked if it was okay if he sat down.

I shrugged. "Sure. Be my guest."

Unlike René, I'm pretty relaxed around guys. That's why they always like to confide in me, I suppose, and ask me fascinating questions, mostly like do I think so-and-so would go out with them. I've never had a real boyfriend, in the romantic sense of the word. When Heather was my age, she'd had dozens of them. I heard my mother tell my father once that I certainly wasn't the boy-bait that Heather was. That phrase, *boy-bait*, made me feel like throwing up, even though I knew it was just common beauty parlor talk. I secretly hated my mother for about a week after that insulting remark, and I became even more resistant to her constant suggestions that I have my hair done in one of the more faddish styles. Mom's a beautician, and she and Heather have always made a good team. Before Heather went away to school, the two of them used to spend hours together with curlers and blow dryers, making real *boy-bait* (ugh!) out of Heather.

Rocky sat down at my table with a carton of popcorn, two humongous root beers, and the beat-up paperback book he was reading before. He set the popcorn in the center of the table and one of the drinks right in front of me.

"For me?" I asked. "Gee, thanks." I closed my history book, but I kept my place with my thumb.

"Have some popcorn," he said, giving it a little nudge.

"Thanks."

"What school do you go to?"

"Me?" I answered, closing my book completely now. "Lincoln. What about you?"

"I *knew* I've seen you there! I go to Lincoln, too."

"Really? I've never seen you. I don't think."

"Isn't your locker over by the *Nugget* office?" I nodded.

"Well, that's where I've seen you, then."

"Wait a minute," I said. "What's your last name?"

"Nevin."

"Well, how about that? So you're Rocky Nevin on the *Nugget* staff." I took a handful of popcorn. "Boy, you guys on the paper sure make me sick. The only people who ever got their names in that thing are on the staff."

He laughed. "Not always. Here, I'll prove it. Tell me your name and I'll work it into the next issue."

"My name is Cairo Hays," I answered, "but don't bother putting it in the paper. I'm not some kind of publicity hound."

"Cairo Hays," he repeated, sounding it out slowly, as if he could taste it. "That's beautiful. *Really* beautiful. How do you spell it? *H-A-Z-E*, as in smog?"

"Nope," I said, shaking my head and looking straight into those amber brown eyes. "It's *H-A-Y-S*, as in horses."

Neither one of us would turn away. Finally, after I don't know how long, we both started laughing, and something about the way he held his head back and shut his eyes when he laughed just made me feel good all over.

I was just starting to drift off to a pleasant sleep, lying peacefully on my side, thinking of large root beers in Styrofoam cups and Rocky Nevin's eyes, when suddenly—don't ask me why—I was wide-awake, up on one elbow, breaking out in a sweat and remembering what my cousin Jerry Spender's mother actually said to me that day so long ago (after I accidentally ground up her little boy's fingers in the blender). What she said was that I was a stupid little bastard and a misbehaving ugly brat, and that she never wanted to lay eyes on me or any of my family ever again.

3

When I was in the third grade and Mercedes started kindergarten, Mom decided she'd better go back to work, so she got her old job back at Yolanda's Beauty Salon, and we had to go to Mrs. Beeker's house every day after school. René went there with us, since her mother had just started working, too, at Tom Bunney's first little copy shop, a tiny kiosk located in the Thrifty Drugstore parking lot. It was called Bunney's Rapid Copies and Newsstand (Copies Kwik as a Bunney and Newspapers from All Over). Since then, René's mother has married Mr. Bunney, and now they have quite a big business going, with four large outlets scattered around town and about fifteen employees.

Mrs. Beeker, the baby-sitter, had four boys of her own. Their names were Craig, Robert, Billy, and Roger. Billy was the one who always went to the bathroom under the porch. I saw him do it once, and I told René about it and we went spying on him. After he finished, René said, "Boy! Now *that's* a handy thing to take on a picnic!" I just about died laughing. René always says the funniest things, and for a long time I thought that she made them up. Now I realize she always has a source. I know that because she still says funny things, but I usually find out later that she heard them on television or read them in the *Reader's Digest*. I was changing the light bulb in the kitchen once when she was over, and she snapped her fingers and said (as if she had just thought it up), "Hey, Cairo. How many flies does it take to screw in a light bulb?" I shrugged and said, "I don't know. How many?"

"Two," she answered slyly. (It was a little embarrassing, because I didn't get it at first. I wasn't expecting anything like that.) That night I asked Mercedes the same thing, and she turned away and said, "Jeez, Cairo, Crystal Boyers told me that one six months ago." So that's how I knew René didn't make *that* up.

It was just before the first lunch period at school, and the corridor was noisy and full of kids rushing every which way. I was standing near my locker with René when I felt someone tapping me on the shoulder. I turned around and saw it was Rocky Nevin! He smiled at René, at the same time gently pulling me over to one side.

"There's a party," he said, raising his voice above the din in the hallway. "Friday night. Mostly *Nugget* staff kids. It's going to be at Allison Ryan's house. She says she knows you. You're invited, if you want to come."

"Allison Ryan?" I repeated, flustered. "Oh,

yeah. She's in my gym class," I added quickly, trying to pull myself together. I couldn't believe Rocky Nevin was actually inviting me to a party! (Of course, he wasn't offering to pick me up, but at least he was telling me about it.) But now I was in a fine pickle! I really wanted to go to that party, just to be around Rocky and get to know him better, but like a big dummy I had just broadcasted the fact to all my friends that I hated parties and wasn't going to go to them anymore. And there was René, watching me with her arms folded, just *waiting* to hear what I would say.

"Gosh, Rocky," I said finally, "see, I don't *go* to parties—anymore—I mean, like the last one I went to, well, I decided I really didn't have that great a time, so . . ." I felt like such a nut, standing there telling him that.

But Rocky's eyes seemed to catch fire. "You don't like parties? Is that what you're saying?"

I shrugged. "Well, yeah. That is, I mean . . ."

He interrupted again. "You don't like parties because somebody's always getting drunk and falling down, and the music's so loud you can't even have a decent conversation, and couples are always fighting about something, and people are doing drugs . . ."

I was nodding my head like a woodpecker. "Yeah! Yeah, that's it."

"Well, what do you know," Rocky said simply. "Hey, I'll see you on Wednesday night, huh?" And then he disappeared into the crowd.

René put one hand on her hip. "And who was *that*, may I ask?"

I smoothed my hair back. "Oh, just a kid I know."

"Boy, there you go," she said. "Acting mysterious again. Sometimes you can be a real pill, you know that?" She tried her best to worm more information about him out of me, but I didn't feel like talking about him yet. I wanted to keep him all for myself.

One of my parents' slides from Egypt shows a picture of a young Muslim boy of eight or nine. He's smiling ever so slightly (like the Mona Lisa) directly into the camera. It's a picture that once you see, you can never forget. The boy is caught forever, stopped in time, with that exquisite expression of simple innocence.

My parents said he had followed them for blocks, begging to have his picture taken. They finally obliged, and as soon as the shutter clicked, the little guy stuck out his hand and demanded, "Baksheesh!" (*Baksheesh* is a word they use a lot in Egypt. It means sort of like a tip.) My parents said they were very surprised at this sudden turnaround.

But the picture is really very nice.

It was garbage day and the guys came around about six in the morning, banging the cans and then running that huge machine that grinds everything up right under my window. On top of that, old Bribe started barking up a storm. I went to the bathroom and then got back in bed, but I couldn't fall asleep.

I got dressed, without washing or anything, and quietly let myself out the back door. It was real humid, practically raining a kind of misty spring rain, and everything smelled sweet and earthy. The garbage men had passed by then, and Bribe was lying on the doorstep with his head between his paws, just gazing at his little doggy world. He seemed genuinely happy to see me, licking my hands and jumping up to my chest. "No, no! Bad dog!" I half-whispered. "Come on. I've got an idea. Let's go for a *walk*. *Walk*, Bribe? Want to go for a *walk?*" He ran around in a crazy circle, and then made a beeline for the garage and the nail where his leash is hung.

We headed out for the street, with Bribe more or less pulling me along, as usual. By the time we got to the school, he had calmed down some, and I let him take up all the slack on the leash so he could nose around every bush and tree. There was a stray dog running loose, and old Bribe's tail started wagging and he started bounding off toward the other dog. I was amazed at his strength, and I was barely able to hold him back. Luckily, the other dog disappeared behind a fence.

On the way home, he stayed closer to me, and I could touch the silky fur on his back with the tips of my fingers. When we got home, I gave him some fresh water, which he drank, and then I sat down on the doorstep. He went sniffing around the side of the house for a few minutes, and then came back to where I was sitting and plopped himself down on my shoes. We sat there together for about five minutes before he got up and wandered off to the garage. My feet were all warm from the heat of his body.

Something really strange and upsetting happened between Aunt Lucille and me. She had called me up—like she does sometimes—and asked if I wanted to go pick a movie video and then go over to her place to watch it. (After her divorce, she moved back with Grandmother and Grandfather Hays, and the first thing she did was talk them into getting a VCR. I don't think my grandfather approves of her moving back with them, especially since he's retired now. You can just tell it in lots of little ways.)

Well, Lucille came and picked me up and she seemed okay then. We talked about different things on the way over to Couch Potato Video, and once we got inside I started to go with her to the comedy section, but I saw this guy there, Peter Lyons, that I knew from school, and I stopped to talk to him. He was there with his older brother, who's out of high school now.

I thought Peter Lyons was good-looking, but his brother! I mean, wow! I don't know how we got on the subject, but they started telling me about a strange old Steve Martin movie, *Pennies from Heaven*, they had seen recently, and how the musical numbers were such great parodies of some of the real old-time Hollywood musicals. Peter even began to demonstrate one of them, and we were all laughing and having a great time.

After I don't know how long, I happened to glance up and there was Lucille, leaning against the wall with her arms crossed and her fingers drumming impatiently on her elbow. She always carries this giant shoulder-strap purse made out of tapestry material to carry candy bars and sandwiches in (I'm not kidding), and I guess the tape was in there and she was ready to leave.

I told the guys I had to go, and I went over and said, "Gee, I'm sorry you were waiting. I didn't know you were finished. What'd you get?"

She didn't even answer me, and I followed her out to the parking lot without either one of us talking.

She started the car and drove for a couple of blocks in a really agitated way. She slammed on the brakes so hard at one stoplight that her purse slid off the backseat and you could hear all the stuff rolling around on the floor mats back there.

Finally she said, "Damn you, Cairo! You're really an inconsiderate brat, you know that?"

Well, that really hurt, coming from her, and I didn't know what to say. She was starting to cry, and in a few seconds she was crying so hard I thought she was going to get in a wreck or something.

We were on one of the avenues by then and there wasn't any traffic, but just the same it scared me. "Pull over, will you?" I said. "Come on, Lucille. You can't drive while you're crying like that."

Luckily, she pulled over to the curb and stopped the car. She leaned on the steering wheel and buried her head in her arms and mumbled, "I'm sorry, Cairo. I'm really sorry." After a minute she raised up her head and looked at me and added softly, "I really shouldn't take it out on you, but I just get so miserable sometimes, I . . . I . . . just . . ."

"Well, it was my fault," I broke in quickly, suddenly realizing how she must have felt left out while I was talking to Peter and his brother. "I shouldn't have ignored you like that—just talking to those kids and letting you go find the movie all by yourself. It really *was* inconsiderate of me."

"Don't be stupid," she said, blowing her nose. "The simple truth is, I was just flat-out jealous of you. You and those boys—talking and laughing like you were."

Then she gave her head a little shake, as if she were trying to shake all those bad feelings out or something, and started up the motor again.

We drove on for a block or so, and then she did what Mercedes would call a "typical Lucille," one of those little things she does that makes us all love her so much; she reached over and gave me a friendly little cuff on the ear and said, "Besides, they were both *way* too young for me anyway, weren't they?"

I just laughed politely, relieved that the little scene was over, but I knew how much she was really hurting inside.

My father read about a photo contest and is going to enter the picture of the little Muslim boy. The contest is only for pictures taken outside of the continental USA. The grand prize is an all-expense-paid trip for the whole family to Disney World, Florida, a place I've always wanted to see. (Unlike Heather, whose impossible dream has always been to take a trip to Hawaii and meet Luana, a pen pal she's had since the fourth grade.)

Only, I read the fine print in the contest rules, and Rule 7 says that the picture must have been taken outside the continental USA *within the last twelve months*. I pointed that fact out to my father, but he said, "Hell, how are they going to know?"

God, I was so shocked. "That's not the point, Dad," I said. "If it says in the rules . . ."

He put the paper down. "Listen, Cairo," he said. "Some people can afford to go out of the country every year, some twice a year, and that's fine. But we can't. Your mother is a beautician and I'm a computer programmer, and we've got three daughters to put through school and a thirty-year mortgage on the house. I happen to have taken a very good photograph I don't know how many years ago on my one and only trip out of the country." He paused. "How else would we ever get a trip to Disney World? Tell me that. The rule is not fair, and it doesn't make any sense."

"Well," I said softly, "if they ask me about it, I'm sure not going to lie."

"They won't ask you. You don't have to worry about that."

I could tell he was angry by the way he raised the newspaper and gave it a little snap before he started reading it again.

I just couldn't stay in the same room with him after that. In a way I agreed with him about the rule—it really *didn't* seem fair—but all the same it still would be lying. The thing is, I've always respected my dad; it was like he was always there for me to depend on, but now, all of a sudden, something had happened. I know it's stupid, but I got kind of a panicky feeling in my chest, and I felt like I might start to cry. Without even thinking where I was going, I went out the back door and whistled softly for Bribe. He came crawling out of his doghouse like a sleepy child, but when he saw me sitting on the steps he was suddenly wide-awake, his tail wagging so hard it made his whole body writhe and twist around like a serpentine. After a minute he calmed down a bit and came and sat beside me. I just threw my arms around him and buried my head in the soft fur around his neck.

I got a short letter from my cousin Margaret. She works in San Francisco for a big restaurant-supply outfit and is active in the Junior Chamber of Commerce and the Young Republican's Club. The letter was typed on company stationery, so she probably wrote it at work. She's kind of conceited, actually, and I don't like her much. She's always talking about some fabulous new guy she's dating, and what a turkey the last one was, as if he were chosen for her by someone else. Anyway, Margaret had to go to Berkeley on business, and while she was there, she dropped in on Heather. She also met Allan. This is what Margaret wrote:

Somebody better do something about Heather, and quick. That Allan Allen character spells trouble with a capital T. He seems like a real wacko to me, and I can't believe Heather is actually planning on marrying him. All he talked about the whole time was pollution, the environment, his sign(!) and the evils of big business. Sometimes I think Heather doesn't have a brain in her head. Please don't show this to your mother, Cairo. I don't want to worry her. I'll talk to you later.

Love, Margaret.

P.S. I must admit, though, he's terribly good-looking!!

I didn't show the letter to Mom, but I did let Mercedes read it.

"What'll we do?" I asked.

She shrugged and turned away, but I know she was beginning to stew about it, too.

Thank goodness I got that name tag for Bribe, because he escaped through a hole in the fence and got all the way to Montgomery Street. Some little kid called from there and said they could bring him back if I wanted. Since I was the only one home, I said yes, that would be great. I didn't even know Bribe had gotten out! I went outside and checked the fence all around (at first I thought someone had carelessly left the gate open) but sure enough, there were three loose pickets along the side by the Goldsmiths' house. While I was waiting for the people to bring him back, I moved the garbage can over to the fence and patched it up that way.

A man and his son (the kid who called, I guess) soon drove up in an old Pinto. The kid opened the car door and Bribe immediately jumped out and, of all things, just ignored me and started running off down the street. It made me feel like two cents. I clapped my hands and called, "Bribe! Bribe! You come back here!"

Bribe just kept running down the street toward the school where I always take him walking. I was so frustrated I actually began to cry. But the man put the car in gear and leaving his kid standing on the lawn next to me, followed Bribe down the street. The car swerved a little, and I could see the man leaning across the seat and opening the door on the passenger side. Then he whistled sharply, and Bribe turned and ran toward the car and jumped right in. I breathed a huge sigh of relief. The man grabbed Bribe by the collar and picked up speed and the car door shut by itself. He made a U-turn and returned to my house. This time he left my dog in the car and got out and walked around to the passenger side to let him out. He held onto his collar while he walked him over to me and said, "Real rover, ain't he, miss?" Bribe's tail was wagging like anything. I felt like smacking him, but, God, I was so relieved to have him back safely. I offered them a reward, and the kid's eyes kind of lit up, but the father just smiled and shook his head and said, "That's mighty kind of you, but we were happy to do it." Then he tousled his little son's hair and off they drove.

Grandpa B said he'd fix the hole in the fence. He lives at a senior citizens' residence called Regal Oaks Manor. My mom found it. Grandpa B is one of those old-fashioned helpless males, and when Grandma B passed away, he wanted to come and live with us, since he "doesn't know how" to cook and "doesn't know how" to clean and "doesn't know how" to pick up after himself. But my mom said, "No way, José," and went shopping around and found Regal Oaks. You have to be over sixty-two years old to live there. They serve one to three meals a day (your choice) and have "light" maid service once a week. What my mom does is go over every once in a while and change his bed sheets and put out clean towels for him and make sure he hasn't run out of toilet paper and denture powder. He can certainly afford to hire someone to do all that stuff, but he prefers that Mom do it.

Compared to the other residents, Grandpa B is in amazing physical condition. He still drives his truck (he used to be a building contractor), and he stores all his old tools in our garage. Nobody knows for sure how much money he has, but he owns several parcels of property around town, and Mom says he's loaded, just like Uncle Larry.

The day he fixed the fence, I went over with Mom to his place to change the sheets and stuff. The oldest living person I ever saw went up in the elevator with us. She was practically bent in half, leaning on her walker, and the way her head was raised and with that humped back and frizzy gray hair, she really reminded me of some kind of barnyard fowl. But then she smiled at me, and I felt guilty for comparing her to a turkey, even though I couldn't help it. She squinted at Mom through her half-inch-thick glasses and said in a croaky but friendly old voice, "Are you just moving in, dearie?" I wish I had a picture of the expression on Mom's face. I had to spend the whole time while we were changing the sheets reassuring her that she certainly didn't look anywhere *near* sixty-two years of age. By the time we were ready to leave, she was able to joke about it, though. At least I hope she was joking. What she said was, "If any more of those old biddies on the elevator ask me if I'm just moving in, I'm going to poke them right in the eye."

One of the funny stories my parents brought back from their trip to Egypt is called "The Mosquito" and it goes like this: On their final evening there, they were strolling down a little side street in Cairo just off the Corniche, enjoying for the last time the exotic sights and sounds of a city they had come to love. (The Corniche is the street that runs right alongside the Nile.) It was all very pleasant and memory making, except for the mosquitoes, which were really going after my father like there was no tomorrow. (My mother is never bothered by mosquitoes; she thinks it's because she takes a daily vitamin supplement, but that is neither here nor there.) Pretty soon my father couldn't stand it anymore, so they went into a shop about the size of a large closet that looked like it could possibly be some kind of Egyptian drugstore.

"Do you have mosquito repellent?" my father asked politely.

Alas, the proprietor did not speak English. He called out to someone in the back, and a woman emerged from behind a curtain.

"Do you have mosquito repellent?" my father repeated, this time slapping one forearm with his hand, pantomiming the murder of an imaginary mosquito.

The woman glanced at her husband, and they both looked puzzled. Two little girls now shyly emerged from behind the curtain.

My father elaborated on his little pantomime by adding a buzzing mosquito, formed by pressing his thumb and forefinger together and raising his hand in a high arc, the whole performance accompanied by a *buzzz-buzzz* sound and ending, as before, with a firm slap on the wrist.

The two little girls were staring, wide-eyed now, and one of them lowered her head and made a tiny giggle. The only responses from the proprietor and his wife were a blank stare and a shake of the head.

"Mosquitoes! Mosquitoes!" my father said

loudly, as he was starting to get agitated. (When he told this story, I could just picture him there. He loses his patience pretty quickly sometimes, but then in a few minutes he gets control of himself.) When he saw he wasn't making any headway, he got another idea. He curled the fingers of his right hand around an imaginary spray can, moved his thumb up and down as if he were depressing the spray valve, and looked imploringly at my mom. *"Pooosbhh,"* he said, walking around the small room, spraying every imaginary and real mosquito in sight.

Now my mother joined in. "There's one!" she said, forming a mosquito with her fingers as my father had done a moment before. *"Buzzz-buzzz,"* she hissed, landing on my father's arm. He whacked himself again, and my mom let her head drop to one side and fluttered her eyelids—her imitation of a dying mosquito.

By now the whole Egyptian family was staring in rapt amazement.

My parents gave up in defeat. They shook hands with the proprietor and his wife, smiled at the little girls, and walked out.

After they were back on the street, my mother turned to look through the window of the little shop. She said she saw the father slapping his wrist and smiling, while the little girls were rolling on the floor with laughter, and the mother was dabbing at her eyes with a handkerchief.

Heather called and invited Mercedes and me to

visit her in Berkeley the next day (Saturday) and maybe spend the night. We'd get a chance to meet Allan Allen, and we would have lots of fun, she said. Mercedes and I jumped at the idea, agreeing between ourselves that it would be the perfect opportunity for us to check the guy out, firsthand. Unfortunately, our parents weren't too thrilled with the idea. In fact, at first they just flat-out said no, we couldn't go.

"Why *not?*" I asked impatiently.

We had just finished dinner and Mom and Dad were having coffee. They looked at each other, each hoping the other one would enumerate the reasons, no doubt.

"Because we said so," my father said finally, coming up with the old unimaginative standby.

"That's no reason!" I answered.

Mercedes gave me a warning glance, and then did it her way. First, she smiled slyly at Dad, implying that his answer was just a joke and she was acknowledging it. Then she said to Mom in a nice, reasoned tone, "So, really, Mom. Why not?"

"Well," Mom said, clearing her throat and setting down her cup, "I guess the main reason is that both your father and I work hard all week and look forward to having our Saturdays for ourselves. I have some sewing to do, and your father likes to relax with his . . ."

"Maybe Cairo could drive," Mercedes interrupted calmly. "She does have her license now, and both you guys said she's a good driver."

My parents didn't answer, so Mercedes just

kept talking. "And since it's a weekend, you won't be needing the car, right? And besides, Cairo wants to check out the Berkeley campus."

I started to say something, but Mercedes gave me a kick under the table.

"Remember, she has to decide on her college pretty soon," Mercedes continued, even though I think I told her I had already scratched Berkeley off my list. She raised her hands, palms up. "So see, this would actually *save* you guys a trip."

One look at Mom and I knew we had it made. Just to save face, she asked a few more motherly questions, which Mercedes fielded like a pro. Then Mom sighed and looked questioningly at Dad, who just threw up his hands and opened the paper.

Mercedes winked at me, as if to say, "Easy as pie, when you know how."

4

It turned out we didn't go to Berkeley on Saturday after all. I had to take Bribe to the vet instead. When I went out to feed him that morning, he was sneezing so bad he couldn't even eat. Mercedes came outside to see what was taking so long.

"Oh, he'll be all right," she said. "Let's go."

"No." I shook my head. "I can't go. Look at him. He can't even stop sneezing long enough to eat."

She put her hands on her hips and gave me a disgusted look. "So he's got hay fever. Big deal. Come on, let's go!"

"Mercedes," I said, "will you please shut up?" I took Bribe's head in my hands and tried to look in his nose. He didn't go for that at all. "I've got to call the vet," I said finally.

The vet's office didn't open until nine. I got their answering machine. Mercedes went around the house banging doors and turning the television on and off and generally making a nuisance of herself.

The vet's line was busy until almost twenty after nine, and when I finally got through, her office assistant told me it sounded like a foxtail to her, but the earliest I could bring him in was one-thirty that afternoon, since the vet had some surgery scheduled until then.

Mercedes called Heather and said we couldn't come, all because of "Cairo's dumb dog."

It did turn out to be a foxtail after all. They had to give poor Bribe a sedative in order to get it out. The vet advised me to get all the foxtails out of the yard, as they were murder for dogs.

As soon as we got home from the vet's, I started in on the yard, and then I had a run-in with Dad about it. Apparently, when I pulled the foxtail weeds out, I accidentally pulled some stupid "flowers" that were mixed in with them. At least that's what he thought. He'd been watching golf on TV all day, and when he finally came wandering out to the backyard (beer can in hand) to check his three rose bushes, he said to me, "What the hell have you done to the garden?"

"What garden?" I asked, honestly and sincerely not knowing what he meant.

"What do you mean, *'What garden?'* " He raised his arm in a sweeping gesture toward the area where I had been working, and a little stream of beer shot out of the can. *"This* garden!" he said.

"This mess," I asked, "is a *gar*den?"

"Yes!" he said, glaring at me. "It is! Or rather, it *was!*"

I couldn't believe we were looking at the same yard.

"Jeez, Dad, it was all foxtails! Look at that pile over there. I've been pulling them out all day."

He glanced over at the big pile I had made under the tree and grunted something and walked over to his roses. I went in the house and watched him for a minute through the screen. After he checked his roses, he looked again at the pile of weeds I had made and then went over and rummaged through it with his foot. I knew darned well there weren't any flowers in there.

I made dinner that night. Mom had been spending most of the day catching up on her mending and cleaning the back porch, so she asked me if I would help her out and put a tuna casserole together. Dad wandered in and saw what I was doing and offered to chop the onions. Naturally, I said yes. And then later, just before I went to bed, he asked me if I wanted to go to the flea market with him the next morning. He usually goes with Mom, of course, but she said she had a really rough week, and what she'd love to do is spend her Sunday sleeping until noon. I think Dad asked me as a way of apologizing for hollering at me about the yard.

The problem was I had promised Mercedes I'd go with her to the tennis courts in the morning and help her with her backhand, since her gym teacher was starting up a little middle school tennis team, and Mercedes really wanted to be on it. But Mercedes happened to be in the room when Dad mentioned the flea market, and she spoke up and said it was okay, she could go with Crystal Boyers.

Dad asking me to go to the flea market was really typical of him. I thought about it once and figured out that we usually communicate by actions rather than words. Oh, I know he used *words* to ask me to go to the flea market, but that's not what I mean. Instead of saying, "I'm sorry I yelled at you about nonexisting flowers," he just said, "Hey, do you want to go to the flea market?" The trick with our kind of relationship is that you have to be good at translating actions into words.

He didn't find any new PKG's at the flea market, but I bought some oddly shaped red-and-gold dangling earrings for only a dollar. I didn't know whether to get them or not, but my dad said they looked nice and handed me a dollar bill.

On the way home he wanted to stop at Sears for some rose fertilizer that was on sale. We had to pass through the kitchen appliances department, and I'm not kidding when I say I almost fainted. A lady was demonstrating a Sears blender, and she was making a fresh strawberry milk shake. I felt my knees starting to buckle, and I actually had to lean on the service counter so I wouldn't fall over.

My dad couldn't imagine what was wrong at first. Then he noticed the strawberries and the whirling sound of the blender and he caught on.

"Oh, honey," he whispered. "Come on. It's okay. I never *realized* you still remembered . . ." and he took me by the hand and led me away.

An idea I've had for a long time, that nobody *really knows* anybody, was confirmed.

We got an audio tape in the mail from Berkeley and a short note from Heather that said Allan was "sitting a house" in Monterey, but would be back by Friday, and maybe Mercedes and I could go over on Saturday. She also said that before he left, she made a tape of him singing his newest composition, a song called "The Foster City Blues." We put it on the player and here's what we heard (sung by Allan):

> *Oh, it's hard to be a cowboy*
> *When they ain't no cows to herd*
> *It's hard to be a wrangler*
> *When they've raked up all the turd*
> > *And built a city where the grass grew*
> > *In former days of yore*
> *Oh, it's hard to be a cowboy*
> *And boy, that makes me sore.*

> (Chorus)
> *Them Foster City Blues*
> *Are just too hard to lose*
> *I've tried for weeks to ditch them*
> *Even put them in my shoes*
> *And walked a mile down the road*
> *And hoped I've paid my dues*
> *For the Foster City, Foster City*
> *Foster City Blues.*

I know it sounds highly improbable, since the words of the song are so silly and asinine, but

Heather's Allan has the most beautiful, masculine, wildly sexy, and haunting voice I have ever heard in my entire life.

Wednesday was a shortened day at school because of the annual All City Teachers' Conference. Since there wasn't time to dress for gym, several of us girls talked Ms. Vickers into letting us sit out on the lawn instead of inside in the stuffy gym. While we were out there, Allison Ryan spotted Rocky coming out of the side door of the Student Affairs office and hollered over to him, swinging her arm in a long arc, motioning for him to come over to where we were sitting in a little circle.

"He's on assignment for me," she told us as he was walking over. "The paper's doing a story about the senior class president's plan for renting the Municipal Auditorium for graduation this year, and Rocky's supposed to get the scoop on it."

I know what Allison was doing, and it was pretty typical of her; she was trying to impress us once again with the fact that she was the editor-in-chief of the *Nugget*, even though she was only a junior in school.

"Did you find out anything?" she asked him when he had joined us. "How much is it going to cost? Does the senior class have enough money in its treasury?"

"I've got it all down, Allison," he told her, pointing to the little notebook sticking out of his shirt pocket. "It's all right here."

"Great!" Allison smiled. Then she scooted over

and patted a spot on the lawn beside her. "Are you too good to sit down with us lowly juniors?"

"Probably. But I'll accommodate you this once." Then he looked directly at me and said softly, "Hi, Cairo."

"Hi," I replied.

"So," he said, looking around at all of us in the circle, "big-time seniors next year, at last, huh?"

"Yep!" Allison replied quickly, winking at him. "And guess what? René's the only one who has a date for our Senior Ball!"

When she said that, all of us girls laughed, since René and her date for the Senior Ball had gotten to be kind of a joke. At first she had been so excited about it, she hardly talked about anything else. We all got really sick of it. So then we started making fun of her, and every time she'd start to say something, no matter what the subject, one of us would interrupt and say, "Well, at least *you* have a date for the Senior Ball!" and stuff like that.

"You're the only one who has a date?" Rocky asked, looking at René with raised eyebrows. Then he looked right at me again. "What about you, Cairo?"

I guess I was blushing. I don't know. But I shook my head and shrugged and treated it like it was a big joke. "Heck, I don't care about the dance," I said. "It's that lousy *photograph* of me at the dance that I'm worried about!"

I was surprised when the other girls all laughed at that. I don't know how many of them really had figured that out yet, but I must have struck a vein of truth. Rocky laughed, too, and it seemed to me that he kept watching me all the time he was there. And when he left he looked quizzically at one of the other girls and said, "Say, this *is* Wednesday, isn't it?" Of course, I knew he was sending me a kind of secret signal. I felt like jumping up and down and yelling, "Yippee!"

I felt even better when Allison said he had been talking to her a lot about me lately, asking her things like did I have a boyfriend, and did I like anybody in particular, and would it be okay if he asked me if I wanted to go to her (Allison's) party, and things like that. God, she made it sound like she was a real Cupid's helper. Like, in case a big romance *did* develop, she would be the one responsible for setting up the whole thing. But I was so happy to learn he'd been asking about me, I didn't even care about that.

Like that guy in the poem we read in English who measures out his life with coffee spoons, I was beginning to measure mine out with Wednesdays. That night at the bingo parlor I wore a fairly new red blouse that I'd never even worn to school yet, and the red and gold earrings my dad got for me at the flea market.

The Snack Shack was really busy when Mom and I arrived, and both Rocky and his mother were waiting on customers. Mom went off to her table with the rest of the players, and I headed for my usual spot by the potted plants, but someone was already sitting in my place. It was okay, though, because I just sat at another table where I got an even better view of Rocky.

I opened my English book and started to do my assignment, which was to pick out a few lines from the poems we were studying and write a paragraph on whether or not we agreed with the poet, being sure to give concrete examples. The lines I picked were from a poem by William Cowper (pronounced "Cooper," Ms. Andes says):

> *God moves in a mysterious way*
> *His wonders to perform;*
> *He plants his footsteps in the sea*
> *And rides upon the storm.*

I was surprised, in a way, to read that in my English book, because I had heard that quote before and always thought it was from the Bible. I said in my paragraph that I both agreed and disagreed with it. For a concrete example, I told about how I had come to get that name tag for Bribe, and how it was later responsible for my getting him back. (The way I got it was, first, because the Rogerses ran out of cat food, and second, I was nice and let that lady with the little kids go ahead of me in the line at the grocery store, and third, while I was waiting I read the Milkbone ad in the *Woman's Day*.) The part I agreed with was that it was a pretty "mysterious way" that I finally got the name tag. Then I said the part I didn't agree with was saying that God did it. I said we really couldn't be sure about that. Maybe it was just a string of coincidences.

After I finished my assignment, I put my English book aside and noticed that there was part of a coffee-stained morning newspaper on the empty chair beside me, so I picked it up and looked at that for a while. I read an interesting article about a book called *The Blackmail Diet*, by John Bear. This is how the Blackmail Diet works: Let's say I wanted to lose ten pounds, for example. I'd give a substantial amount of money (for me, right now, that would be about five dollars) to somebody like Mercedes or René to hold, and then we'd draw up a sort of contract. If I didn't lose the ten pounds by the time I said I would, Mercedes or René would have to give the money (anonymously) to somebody like the Rogerses, for instance—so *they could get more cats to mistreat!* Anyway, that's the idea. If I don't lose the weight, the money goes where you specify—for something (or to somebody) you really *hate*. The article in the paper quoted a woman who said it had worked for her. She said the power of hate should never be underestimated.

My reading was interrupted by a shrill voice calling out, "Bingo!"

As usual, that happy cry was followed by a universal groan, "Oh, no!" One elated person, I thought, but a whole roomful of disappointed ones. And then my mom won the next one! I couldn't believe it. Actually, though, it's not too surprising, since her "system" consisted of getting an additional card for every night she didn't win. She had cards spread out all over the place. The prize was $250.

I left my books at my table and rushed over to where she was sitting and congratulated her. I didn't spoil her fun by asking if she was "ahead" now, because I knew she'd already spent more than $250, if you counted all the cards she'd bought since we started coming. I may be a misbehaving ugly brat, but I'm certainly not a spoilsport.

Just before the intermission, I went to the ladies' room and combed my hair, and then I walked up to the Snack Shack to get my root beer. Rocky's mom started to wait on me, but he swooped over and grabbed her two arms from behind and moved her over to one side, saying in a humorous way, "Thank you, Mom, but I'll get this one."

She turned her head and looked up at him and said, "Oh?" Then she smiled at me and disappeared into the little room in back.

"Was that your mother who got a bingo earlier?" he asked. "I saw you go over to her table."

"Yep. That was her, all right." I shrugged and smiled helplessly. "I don't know why, but she just likes to play bingo."

"Some people do," Rocky answered matter-of-factly. He placed my root beer on the counter, and I paid him for it.

"Hey, I like those earrings," he said, reaching out to touch one. "They're little silhouette maps of Iberia, aren't they?"

Iberia? That was news to me. I took one off and we examined it together.

"That's what it is, all right," Rocky said. "See? Here's Portugal, and there's Spain. Valencia is way over on the east, and down here is Gibraltar . . ."

"The Rock of Gibraltar?" I interrupted. "That's where it is, in Spain?"

Rocky's face was close to mine. Even his eyelashes were golden brown, like Bribe's. "Are you trying to kid me?" he asked.

Then he looked down at the earring again. "Look here," he said, tracing along one side with his fingernail. "This little line—that's the Portuguese border."

"Rocky?" It was his mother, calling to him from the back room.

"Be right there, Mom," he called out.

"Listen," he said to me, "I've got to help her get ready for the intermission. I'll see you afterward, okay?"

"Okay," I said, trying to sound nonchalant, but feeling my face flush all the same.

When Rocky came to join me, he was carrying his books, two large cartons of milk, and a couple of donuts wrapped up in a napkin. He set them on the table and remarked, "Day-olds. On the house. Your mom get any more bingos?"

"Ha!" I said. I looked at the donuts, sticky with glaze, and picked up a chocolate one. I broke off a piece and was about to take a bite when I happened to turn it over and glance at the underside. A dead fly was stuck to the glaze, wings spread as if it were on exhibit.

"Yuck," I said, and showed it to Rocky.

He grabbed it out of my hand. "Jesus." He was blushing. He quickly wrapped it back up in the napkin and strode over to the nearest waste-basket and threw it in. While he was doing that, I took a fast look at the titles of his books. One was that *Let's Go* book, and he also had a physics text and a book from the library called *Famous Victorian Poets*. He walked back to our table brushing his hands together. While he was examining the remaining donuts, I thought right away about René's flies-in-the-light-bulb joke, and if it had been anyone else but Rocky, I probably would have told it. But I liked this guy too much. I mean, the *last* thing I wanted was for him to get the wrong impression of me. So instead I just laughed and said, "It's obvious you've never been to Egypt!"

He looked down at me, puzzled. "What's that supposed to mean?"

"Well, see, my parents went to Egypt seventeen years ago, and one of the stories they brought back is called "The Fly in the Croissant.""

His eyes were on me and he was following every word.

"Oh, but you don't want to hear about that," I said.

"*Grrr!*" he growled, grabbing both of my wrists and pretending he was going to crush them. "Don't ever *do* that. It drives me *crazy* when people do that."

"Okay, okay." I laughed. "Let go. I'll tell you."

But he didn't let go right away. He held on for just a moment longer, watching me all the while. "Let's hear it then," he said, ending his little pre-

tense of anger with a shy and embarrassed grin.
"Oh, it's really not much of a story," I said,
surprised at my own sudden embarrassment.
"Cairo . . ." he warned slowly.
"Oh, I'm going to tell you," I said quickly.
"Don't worry." I cleared my throat. "Well, the way
they tell it is that one morning when they were
having breakfast (in their cheap little hotel off the
beaten track), the waiter only brought one croissant
and gave it to my father. After a few minutes, my
father called him over and motioned that my
mother didn't get *her* croissant. The waiter nodded
in a bored and disgusted way and finally went and
got her one. When my mother broke it open, a dead
fly fell out. Then they reenacted the little episode
for the camera and made it into a three-slide production. Slide one shows the waiter's back, slide
two is a picture of the croissant, and slide three
shows a little black speck on the table. That's the
fly."
Rocky stared at me blankly.
"That's it." I shrugged. "I told you it wasn't
much of a story."
"What do you mean? It's a perfect story. I love
stories like that."
"Well, you don't look like you do."
"Because I'm not falling all over myself laughing? Hey, come on, it's not that kind of a story.
The *only* response to a deliciously sarcastic, self-
parodying three-slide-production story like that is a
deadpan stare."
I just looked at him.

"Tell me another one," he demanded. "Tell me another Egypt story. But wait—hold it. *Cairo!* That's why they named you Cairo!"

I nodded. "Good thing they didn't go to Turkey, huh?' It was one of my old standby jokes.

Rocky just groaned.

"You want to hear their mosquito story?" I asked.

"Does Jell-O wobble? Of course I do!"

So I told him about the little Egyptian family having hysterics over my parents' attempts to buy that mosquito spray, and this time he really laughed. After a minute he got serious and said, "Boy!" and shook his head.

"What?" I asked. "Boy what?"

"Oh, I don't know. Egypt. Wow. I'd sure like to see your parents' slides sometime."

I caught my breath. "Don't tell them that. They'd grab you in a minute and then you'd be sorry. You wouldn't see daylight again for three weeks."

"I wouldn't mind. Egypt—well, Egypt's on my list, too, but first I want to see Europe. I want to see the world so bad—Italy, Spain, Denmark, Poland . . ." He reached over and picked up *Let's Go Europe*, the book I had seen him marking up that other time. He flipped the pages, and I saw the words were almost entirely colored by his yellow highlighting pen.

"I know exactly where I'd stay and what I'd do first in every city."

"When are you going? Before college, or what?"

He closed the book and put his physics text and that Victorian poets book on top of it and pushed them all aside. "I don't know," he said brusquely. "I'd like to go this summer, before I get involved in college, but it's that old problem."

"Money," I said.

"That's the one." He sat up straight and took a deep breath. "My mother says I've got the wanderlust." He paused, then added quietly, "She said my father had it, too."

"Did he ever get to go anywhere?"

Rocky started looking away, and he shifted around in his chair. He rubbed his face with his hand and blinked several times. "Not really. Oh, well, my mother told me he went to Mexico and South America—before they were married—but she said he was always talking about . . ." His voice drifted off.

I nodded and made some little response. I had an idea his father was dead.

"My father was one of the last Americans to be killed in Vietnam," he said flatly. "But he got his name engraved on that huge black monument in Washington, D. C. That's something, isn't it?"

How bitter he was! I didn't know how to answer.

"Mom and I finally went to see it last summer. We would have gone sooner, you know, but first we had to save up the money, and then Mom had to arrange to get time off from work, which wasn't so easy. The owner himself had to come in and sub for her."

"Oh yeah? Doesn't she ever get a regular vacation?"

"Oh, sure. The owner comes in. But he's usually on vacation himself during the summer."

"Oh."

"We had a chance to actually *touch* my father's name, you know. On the monument, I mean."

Rocky's face was expressionless. I held my breath. *Rocky Nevin's dark side*, I thought. Well, I *did* want to know him better, I told myself. It looks like I'm getting my wish.

"We even got to take close-up pictures of it," he said. The anguish in his voice seemed to pierce right through my chest. "You see, we had our new Funtime Take-Along camera . . ."

"Stop it, Rocky," I whispered. "Please stop it."

He put both elbows on the table and pounded his forehead with his clenched fists. His eyes were shut tightly in a painful grimace. "I'm sorry," I heard him say with a slight shake of his head. "I'll be okay in a minute."

"Yeah," I said, and I shut my own eyes and waited. When I opened them again (how long—a minute, two minutes?) later, I was shocked at the change that had come over him. His face looked gaunt and pale, except for the redness around his eyes, and his hands were trembling slightly as he reached in his back pocket for his handkerchief.

"Damn! I hate it when I get like this," he said softly. "Just don't pay any attention to me, Cairo."

I reached out and touched his hand for a brief

moment. It felt damp and cold. "It's okay" was all I could say.

"It's just that damned monument," he said with a joyless little laugh. "Just remembering it always affects me this way."

"Well, it must be hard for you, I guess . . ."

Suddenly the color came back in his face. "For God's sake, Cairo, I'm not looking for sympathy!"

"No, no," I protested. "I know that, Rocky."

"It's all just so senseless," he said finally. "Life is insane, really." He raised his head and surveyed the bingo players who surrounded us, all busily searching for little numbers on their cards. "Look at those people, for instance, trying to win money so they can come back next week and lose it. Do you see any purpose to that? Do you see any purpose or meaning to *life*, for God's sake?"

I wished I had an answer that could help him, but I didn't, not really. All I could do was to tell him softly that I've often wondered about that myself, and still haven't come up with an answer. He looked at me and nodded, and we continued to sit there without speaking. After a while, he was somehow able to shake the dark and hopeless mood that had so suddenly overtaken him.

5

It was an unseasonably hot and muggy Saturday when Mercedes and I finally drove over to Berkeley. I had worried about who would feed Bribe the next morning, and was pleasantly surprised when Mom just volunteered to do it. While I was showing her how much to give him, I noticed that she even reached down and petted him a couple of times. Old Bribe was jumping around us like crazy, probably thinking he was going to get an extra feeding that day.

"I mean," Allan Allen was saying, "take dirt, for example." He leaned forward, looking at us all in turn, but finally settling his intense gaze on me. "Just plain, old, everyday *dirt*."

Mercedes and I, along with Allan and Heather and four or five other people, were sprawled around on the upstairs porch at Frogpond. It was evening and the smell of jasmine was gently wafting through the air. Heather had confided to us earlier that she had, in effect, moved in at Frogpond, but there was no sense telling that to Mom, as it would serve no useful purpose.

"Dirt?" I asked, putting one leg up on the railing and reaching for another handful of homemade tahini poppy seed granola.

"Just plain, old, everyday dirt, Allan?" Mercedes repeated super-innocently in a tone I recognized all too well.

"Do you all realize that when you put a seed— any old seed, mind you—in just plain everyday dirt, it *grows?*" Allan continued. "Dirt contains all the ingredients necessary for the sprouting and growth of that seed. Dirt is nature's perfect food." He took a deep drag on whatever it was he was smoking. "It's so marvelous. Just incredibly marvelous when you take the time to think about it."

A guy in a cutoff T-shirt and baggy drawstring pants stood up and stretched and wandered off.

"And do you know what they're doing to that dirt?" Allan continued angrily. "They're paving it! That's what! They're making subdivisions, and shopping centers, and stupid arcades. They're making nuclear power plants, that's what!"

"Allan gets really excited about stuff like that," Heather chimed in, patting him across his shoulder blades. "Don't you, honey?"

"What's an arcade, anyway?" a feminine voice asked from somewhere almost out of earshot.

Nobody bothered to answer.

"I just don't think they should pave all the dirt, that's all," Allan concluded with an injured air.

"That's right," Mercedes agreed, tossing an

empty soda pop can in my lap. "If they pave all the dirt, how the heck can the seeds grow? Right, Allan?"

"That's it," he said. "You can just bet your little booties on that!"

That night, sleeping on a couch in the TV room at Frogpond, I had my dream again—the one in which I discover a way to turn back the clock; to return to and alter the past. But in my dream, something always prevents me from writing down the formula. This time, whenever I would start to write, my pencil would fall into the blender and be ground into sawdust. I'd grab a new pencil, and the same thing would happen all over again. So when I woke up, the secret had once again been left behind in another world.

The next morning Allan punched a window out with his fist. It was just a small pane, but it shattered glass all over the place. Mercedes and I didn't see him do it, but we heard the crash and rushed to the kitchen. He was standing there with kind of a hangdog look, cradling his hand, which, luckily, was not injured. Little splinters of glass were hanging from his clothes, so Heather made him go change while she swept the floor.

The big house was dark and strangely quiet. "Where is everybody?" I asked, as Mercedes and I sat down at the cluttered kitchen table.

"On Sunday mornings you don't see anyone around until noon, usually," she answered, dumping the dustpan into a bag under the sink. Her hair was not combed yet, and for the first time I noticed she had two little lines between her brows.

"Why did he *do* it?" Mercedes whispered softly, asking the question that was on my mind, too.

Heather sat down with us at the table, clearing a place for herself by shoving the newspapers and magazines and half-filled glasses and beer cans off to one side. "Oh, I don't know," she said, tossing her head. "It's like he gets so *frustrated*—at different things in the world, you know—he has to vent out his anger." She shrugged helplessly and gave us a weak smile. "He doesn't mean anything by it."

"Seems pretty stupid to me," Mercedes said with her usual forthrightness.

"It's not *stupid*, Mercedes!" Heather said, her face flushing. "It's . . . it's just the way he is."

"Yeah. Stupid," Mercedes muttered.

"You'd better shut that mouth right this instant!" Heather said, slapping the table with her open palm, making the glasses and cans jump as if they had been stung.

"Will you two cut it out?" I said. "Or else we're getting right in the car, Mercedes, and going straight back home."

That did the trick. Mercedes just let out an exaggerated sigh and turned her back to us, all of a sudden very interested in the posters and stuff hanging all over the kitchen walls.

"So!" I said with false gaiety. "What else is happening around here, Heather?"

Heather quit glaring at Mercedes and pretended

all was well again. "Oh, I don't know." She paused, and then suddenly started up again. "Hey, Cairo, do you remember Dawn?"

I caught my breath. "Who?"

"Our cousin Dawn. Do you remember her?"

There seemed to be a sudden weakness around my shoulders. "Well, sure, I—"

"Well, I've started writing to her! I thought this silly family feud has gone on long enough."

"Silly family feud?"

"That business with Jerry's fingers! I mean, you didn't know what you were doing! You were just a kid! So one day I wrote to Dawn—she's my age, you know—and now we've corresponded three or four times. I've got her letters someplace. Oh, I guess they're still at my old apartment. Anyway, I called her on the phone last week, and told her about . . ." She stopped a second, glancing at Mercedes. ". . . about Allan. I even talked to Aunt Ginger—she's *really* nice, Cairo—and invited them all to my wedding. By the way, did I tell you we should know any day now about the Fourth of July? Dr. Gabriel is going to be out of the country during June and July, but he said he'd be sure to check the charts for us this week, so we'd know in plenty of time."

"Oh, *really!*" Mercedes said. "*Fascinating!*"

"Mercedes!" Heather warned. "Watch it! Just keep quiet now, will you please."

Could it be possible, I thought. Could it be possible I might have to face them all again? I was about to ask Heather if Aunt Ginger *accepted* her invitation, but just then Allan ambled back into the kitchen. Heather greeted him with a big smile and quick kiss on the lips. She rummaged around in the freezer and found a package of eight-grain muffins, which she put in the microwave while Allan made hobo coffee. That's what he called it, anyway. He just boiled a pot of water and threw in a handful of coffee. They had an old strainer hanging on the wall that they strained it with, and it was the most terrible stuff I ever tasted.

Then they read their horoscopes in the *Berkeley Bugle*. Dr. Gabriel ("Stargazing with Gabe") told Heather to *"set aside time for shopping,"* and Allan's advice was, *"A take-charge day for you, and a perfect time to entertain out-of-town visitors. Keep expenses down, if possible."* So Heather said she would go to the store while Allan took us for a walk. Everything would work out perfectly, she said.

Allan put his hand on Heather's forearm. "Hey, get me some prawns at the store, babe. That big frozen kind."

From where I was sitting, I had a clear view of Heather's face. "Gosh, Allan," she said, trying to smile, "I don't think I can. See, when I wrote that last check to Dr. Gabe, I only had about eight dollars left in the checking account."

Allan's grip tightened on Heather's arm. "This is my take-charge day," he said. I could tell he wasn't joking around. "So get me some prawns, okay?"

Heather actually winced, and I thought I saw real fear in her eyes. Allan wouldn't let go of her arm, and there was an intensity between them that sent a chill through me. I suddenly felt that here was a genuine disaster waiting to happen, and I couldn't just stand idly by and watch.

Finally, Heather scraped back her chair and freed herself from his grasp. She murmured something like, "Well, maybe there's some change in my old pair of jeans."

Mercedes had been thumbing through a magazine, watching this little scene between Heather and Allan out of the corner of her eye. She looked up now and remarked casually, "You guys can't really *believe* that stuff."

"What stuff's that?" Allan asked.

"All that *this-is-your-take-charge-day* stuff. All that horoscope crap, to put it mildly," Mercedes said.

Heather and Allan exchanged exasperated expressions, and then Allan sort of waved his hand in the air, as if to say, "Well, she's your sister. You explain it."

Heather sat back down at the table. She choked back her last swallow of coffee and quickly set the mug down on the sticky table. "You just don't understand, Mercedes," she started. "See, millions of people believe in astrology, from movie actors and presidents' wives to doctors and lawyers and merchant chiefs, even." She smiled and shrugged. "We're in good company. What else can I say?"

"But it's so stupid!" Mercedes exclaimed, losing her temper a bit now. She reached for the newspaper. "Listen to this. Here's what it says for Virgo:

'*Seek expert's advice on remodeling plans. Delay planned automobile trip. Mate could be on the cranky side.*' " She threw down the paper. "What crap! One out of twelve persons is a Virgo, right? More or less—one out of twelve. You mean to say that advice fits all of them? Don't you see how that is so—"

"Aha!" Heather exclaimed, interrupting her, "Listen to this, smart ass! When Dr. Gabriel writes his column, he consults *my* personal chart for his advice to Gemini's and *Allan's* personal chart for Leo's!"

"What do you mean?" Mercedes asked impatiently. "How could he do that?"

"Dr. Gabriel is a *local person*, Mercedes!" Heather started to explain.

"And Heather and I are his best clients!" Allan finished triumphantly.

"I don't get it," I said. "You mean when he writes his column, he's really writing your *personal* predictions?"

"That's right!" Allan said gleefully. "As a special favor to us, too! Can you beat that! He said he had to base them on somebody's actual charts, and for just a small extra charge, he said he'd use ours!"

"And what's so great about it," Heather added, "is that since he goes out of town so frequently, we still have the benefit of accurate predictions!"

"Well, I still don't see how you can believe that garbage," Mercedes persisted. "It's *pseudo*science, for God's sake. It even says so in the dictionary. It's like biorhythms, and channeling. It's all just bunk!"

Allan brushed back his mane of disheveled black

hair. With those dark blue eyes and heavy lashes, he looked like a fugitive from *Playgirl* magazine. "The question is not only believing, Mercedes, but also in trying to live harmoniously with the larger, universal plan of the cosmos. To put it simply," he added with a smirk, "we don't like to rock the cosmic boat, see? We just like to go with the flow."

"The cosmic boat, huh? Does that include punching out windows?" Mercedes asked sweetly.

Allan took a deep breath and stretched, slowly raising his fists to the ceiling, and put on a silly, sheepish expression, while Heather came swiftly to his defense.

"Now just a minute, Mercedes," she said firmly. "Allan was very upset this morning. The County Planning Commission is considering rezoning some farmland over by the airport—"

"And we're not going to let them get away with it!" Allan declared.

He looked so handsome and dedicated for a moment there, I could almost understand why Heather was infatuated with him, even though I knew he was a complete saphead and the worst possible choice for a husband.

A few minutes later, after Allan had left the room, Mercedes stood up and kind of hovered around Heather's chair. Then she leaned over Heather's shoulder and started brushing some crumbs off the table or something. I don't know exactly what she was doing. "What's the matter?" Heather asked her. "What are you doing?"

Mercedes didn't answer for a minute. Then she

said, "You know, Heather, if you marry that guy, well, I think you'd be making a big mistake."

Heather's face actually turned purple. Shades of red and purple. "Why you little know-it-all!" she said. "Anytime I need advice from a little pip-squeak like you, I'll be sure to let you know! But until then, just mind your own damn business!"

"Hey, come on," I said, pulling on Mercedes's arm. "We have to get ready to go on that walk with Allan, remember?" I looked at Heather. "And you have to go to the store."

Heather was still glowering at Mercedes. "Not until she promises to keep her juvenile and half-baked opinions to herself! I don't have to listen to that!"

"Okay. Okay," I said, playing peacemaker again. "She won't do it anymore. Will you, Mercedes?"

"No," Mercedes said simply, acting (I thought) surprisingly grown-up. "But I had to say it at least once."

Heather left for the store, grim-faced, while Mercedes and I returned to the TV room to pack our pajamas back in our overnight bag.

"Well, at least I tried," Mercedes said quietly, as soon as we were alone.

"Yeah," I whispered back. "I noticed."

"It would be a disaster for Heather to marry that clown. Did you see the way he was squeezing her arm? He was really hurting her." Mercedes shook her head. "But, God," she said. "I don't know. I really don't know. Heather is an adult.

What else can we do? She sure doesn't listen to *me!*"

I was tying my shoelaces in double knots, the way I always do before going on a long walk. "Well, listen," I said. "First things first. Like, what are we going to do with Allan all morning, anyway? What are we going to *say* to this guy?"

A sudden knock on the door made us both jump. "You girls ready to go?" It was Allan.

"Yes, Allan!" I called out. "Just a second." I looked up at Mercedes. "Whew!" I whispered, wiping my forehead.

"Let's just try to play it cool," Mercedes suggested in my ear. "I mean, we can't change him, that's for sure. Let's just go along with him. Let's just pretend he's normal and see what happens."

"Can you believe this is happening?" I whispered back. *"Pretending* our future brother-in-law is *normal!"*

A few minutes later we were walking along Hearst Avenue with Allan, going toward town, headed for his favorite espresso house. Suddenly, looming right ahead of us was something I'd never even known existed—an idea so elementary in its simplicity, yet so unusual and unique it had me gaping. It was a park, for *dogs!* But Mercedes and Allan wouldn't even stop walking. "Wait!" I said. "Look! It's a park—for *dogs!*"

"Cairo, come *on!*" Mercedes hollered. "We don't want to look at any dumb dogs."

But I was inside the fenced park by then. A beautiful collie had come up to me and was licking my hand. I walked back over to the gate with the collie at my heels and called out to Allan, cupping my hands around my mouth. "I want to stay here, Allan. Pick me up on your way back, okay?"

He waived airily over his shoulder, and he and Mercedes kept on walking up the street.

I quickly counted seven dogs running loose in the park, barking, frolicking with each other, chasing balls and Frisbees. Several people were sitting at a picnic table way at the other end of the large grassy expanse, and I walked over to them. One woman was knitting at the table, and a couple of guys were resting under a tree. A boy about my age was tossing Frisbees and balls as fast as the dogs would retrieve them. A white Scottie and some kind of toy poodle were chasing each other around in circles, and a huge German shepherd was cautiously sniffing a tiny fluff-ball of a dog about one-eighth his size.

I sat down next to the knitting lady, who smiled at me and moved her stuff to make more room for me. "Oh, that's okay," I said. "There's a lot of room." I cleared my throat. "Which dog belongs to you?"

She pointed with one of her needles. "The shepherd there. And I also brought my neighbor's Scottie."

I put my knees up to my chest and hugged them, rocking back and forth on the hard bench. "I've just never seen anything like this before. I love it!"

"Oh, yes," the lady said, smiling at my enthusiasm. "It's very nice."

"Do the dogs ever fight?" I asked.

"I've been coming here for a long time, and I've never seen a serious fight. Since the animals are not on leash, they seem to work things out. Dominance is established quickly."

"My dog would love it here. I wish I could bring him someday," I said.

That afternoon a bunch of us from Frogpond went out and picketed some picketers. Allan organized it all. Actually, he was pretty neat. He seemed so different. I began to think I might have overreacted that morning during that little incident at the breakfast table.

What happened was some well-known environmentalist was giving a lecture at the Women's Club about offshore drilling, and Allan had heard that the pro-oil people had hired some kids to picket outside the building where the meeting was going to be held. So Allan went down to the basement and hurriedly slapped some signs together and knocked on everybody's door at Frogpond and managed to get eight or ten people together. Allan brought his guitar, and we sang and marched up and down, insulting the other picketers and generally having a lot of fun. Allan tried to teach us one of the songs he wrote a long time ago, called the "Oil Spill Rag," but the melody was difficult and the words didn't make a lot of sense. Finally, we just sang "We Shall Overcome" about a hundred and fifty times, and, afterward, we went back to Frogpond and drank wine and ate bread and cheese.

We didn't even cut the bread—we just broke off big hunks of it. The same with the cheese.

Later, when we were saying good-bye to Heather, I noticed there were two small bruises on her arm where Allan had gripped her. Once we were in the car, I asked Mercedes if she had noticed them, too. "Did you see those black-and-blue marks on Heather's arm where Allan had squeezed her this morning?" I asked.

Mercedes answer surprised and disappointed me. "I don't want to talk about it now, okay?" she said.

"But, listen, Mercedes, I think we—"

"I said I didn't want to talk about it!" she repeated testily. "So I don't want to talk about it, okay?"

"Well, *par*don me," I answered. "It's not like she's our sister, or anything. It's not like she's about to . . ."

I looked over at Mercedes. She was sitting up straight, just staring ahead at the highway, expressionless. It was her famous sphinx look. I decided I might as well save my breath.

It was late when we finally got back from Berkeley that night. My mom came out of the shower just as I was going to my room.

"Oh, good," she whispered. "You're home. How's Heather?"

I hesitated a second. "She's okay," I whispered back. "I'll tell you about it tomorrow."

She nodded and tightened the belt of her robe.

As I reached for the doorknob, she touched my arm. "I have to tell you, Cairo, we got a surprise phone call yesterday."

I turned to look at her.

"It was your Aunt Ginger."

I think I just stood there with my mouth open.

"Heather and Dawn have been corresponding, and even talking on the phone! Isn't that something!"

Oh boy, I thought. Here it comes.

"It's been such a long time since I've heard her voice." Mom smiled and wiped a tear from her eye, then continued, "Ginger says it's time we buried the hatchet. She even apologized for letting this go on for so long, and said they want to come to our Fourth of July block party and, hopefully, to Heather's wedding." She hugged me briefly. "Isn't that wonderful? It's the best news I've had for months!"

I couldn't answer. All I could think about was Jerry. Little Jerry with the mangled fingers. He was five then, and I was ten. So now he's eleven years old. An eleven-year-old boy with three fingers missing from his right hand, all because of his cousin Cairo, and the astrology column in the morning paper.

6

I got a summer job and didn't even have to go around hunting for one! René fixed it up for me. I'll be working at Bunney's Copy Shop and Newsstand, going around to the various outlets, taking the place of vacationing employees. I figured it out, and I'll make enough money to take care of all of Bribe's needs for at least five years! (Except his food, of course. Mom's still supposed to pay for that.) I start work as soon as school is out. Good old René!

My aunt Lucille called again and we went to Couch Potato Video and got another movie. My grandparents had the popcorn made and the cold drinks set out by the time we got back. The movie (*Lovers and Other Strangers*) was hilarious. It had some very funny sex scenes, which didn't shock me, but sure made my grandparents nervous. I was watching them (my grandparents) out of the corner of my eye. They were almost funnier than the movie. Every time something sexy started to happen on the screen, my grandmother's foot would begin to jiggle, and my grandfather would tap his finger on the arm of his chair. At one point the jiggling and tapping went on for five minutes straight. I started watching her foot and his finger more than the movie.

On the way home, Lucille opened up to me and told me how disgusted she was with herself. A friend at work had told her how she had lost over twenty pounds simply by going on a strict vegetarian diet, and Lucille gave it a try. But it only lasted two days. At the end of the second day she went to Wendy's and ate three hamburgers in less than five minutes.

At first I didn't say anything, but I was thinking about the Blackmail Diet I had read about in the paper, and I was wondering whether or not I should tell her about it.

We were stopped at the light at the intersection of Rand Avenue and E Street, and I turned to look at her. There were tears in her eyes, and her face was contorted with misery.

"Honestly, Cairo," she said, "sometimes I feel so depressed and . . ." she hesitated, "and awful. I . . . just wished I were dead."

When she said that, my whole body suddenly felt limp and cold, and I was really scared. That's when I decided I'd go ahead and tell her.

She practically jumped at the idea. When we got to my house, she insisted on coming in and weighing herself right then and there. Then she wrote out a check to me for five hundred dollars and told me to cash it the next day and put the money in a safe place. She wanted to go for broke—to vow to lose seventy-five pounds, but I told her I didn't think that was a good idea. Actually, I was beginning to have second thoughts about the whole thing. What would happen if it didn't work? If she was depressed now, how would she feel if she failed again?

"Okay," she said excitedly. "Twenty pounds in two months."

"That's still too much," I replied. "You know, Lucille, I wonder if this is such a hot idea after all. I mean, if—"

"Please, Cairo, don't fight me on this. I know I can do it!"

Just one look at her and I realized I couldn't back out now. "Twenty pounds in *three* months then," I said, finally.

She agreed immediately, and we wrote out the deal. It was just as I suspected it would be: If she didn't lose twenty pounds in the next three months, I was to give the cash, anonymously, to her ex-mother-in-law.

I was at the store looking for a folder for my science class report, and I noticed that the Mother's Day cards were already picked over. My gosh! Could it be that Mother's Day was next Sunday? Sure enough, that night my mother made her annual What-I-Expect-to-Get-for-Mother's-Day announcement. Mom has been doing this for as long as I can remember. René thinks it's weird, since her mother absolutely detests Mother's Day and won't have a thing to do with it. That just goes to show how *different* mothers can be. René's mother, for instance, won't even allow her or her little brother to get a card, let alone flowers or candy. I remember when we were in elementary school and our teachers would help us make those stupid little presents—like heart-shaped key holders made out of twisted pipe cleaners, or little pieces of junk glued onto magnets to use as refrigerator note holders—René would always throw hers in the empty lot on the way home from school. She said her mother has always been incensed by the idea that the overwhelming burdens and responsibilities of motherhood should be appreciated for only one crummy day out of the entire year.

My mother has an entirely different philosophy. She says she'll take anything she can get, and really milks it for all it's worth. One year she managed to have Dad dig out all the back lawn and replace it with new sod. It took him three weekends to complete the job. Another time she contracted to have the driveway repaved. Last year she had new linoleum put in the kitchen, and the chimney swept out by two redheaded guys in top hats who sang music from *Mary Poppins* the whole time they were doing the job.

This year, she announced, she wants a "new dining room." By that she means new paint from top to bottom and a new rug. What's more, she said she's sick to death of those ugly purple curtains in there and wants to personally throw them in the garbage can. Dad and Mercedes and I talked it over and decided that Dad will do the walls, Mercedes will help him with the woodwork, and I get to wash the windows inside and out and sew the new curtains. The only concession Mom would make is that we have until the Fourth of July to get the job done.

I drove Mercedes to the Bel Aire Shopping Mall so I could look for some dining room curtain material and she could pick up her new tennis racket, which was being strung at the sports shop. On the way over, I made a really serious driving error and almost scared her pants off. Mine, too. I was making a left-hand turn and just wasn't paying attention to my driving, since I was thinking about Rocky. I forgot that the oncoming cars have the right-of-way. I turned directly in front of this guy, and he missed us by just inches. Naturally, he rolled down his window real fast—after he had screeched to a stop—and swore a blue streak at us. Mercedes was nice about it, though. She leaned over and screamed in my ear, "Cairo, you goddamned fool, you almost got us killed, you know that!"

After we got the curtain material and picked up her racket, I told Mercedes my throat was really dry and let's go get a drink. "I know this guy who works at the Snack Shack," I said in my most ordinary voice.

Rocky was slicing lettuce with his back to the counter when we walked up. I just watched him for a minute, not saying anything. I loved the way he sliced that lettuce.

Rocky's mom saw us standing there, but she must have recognized me, because instead of waiting on us, she smiled and sang out, "Oh, Rocky . . . *cus*tomers!"

Rocky twisted his head to look at us, and I'm almost sure he blushed when he saw who it was. "Oh, hi, Cairo," he said, reaching for a towel and drying his hands. "Gosh, is it Wednesday night already?"

I just laughed and said, "Hi, Rocky. This is my sister Mercedes."

"Hi, Mercedes. Hey, let's see the racket. Is it new?"

Mercedes said hi and handed him the racket. "Yeah. I just got it," she said shyly.

Rocky strummed it like a guitar a couple of times, listening to the sound. "Hmm. Strung pretty tight." Then he grabbed it by the handle and a few short swings. "Boy, you must have a tiny hand!"

Mercedes shrugged and held them out for his inspection.

"Yeah," he said. "They're really small. What is this, about a four?"

Mercedes nodded. "Yes," she said. "A four."

"*Nice* racket," Rocky said, handing it back to her. "Very nice."

"Thanks," Mercedes answered. "You sound like a tennis player."

"Oh, I play a little . . ."

"What do you mean, a *little?*" his mother said, stepping over to join the conversation. "If Rocky didn't have to work, he'd be top man on the team. But since he has to work, he's not on the team at all."

"Oh, Mom . . ." he began.

"Well, it's true . . ."

"Mom, here, she's the *real* pro," Rocky broke in. "The pride of Arizona State, right?"

Mrs. Nevin gave him a friendly little punch on the arm. "I can still give you a run for your money, Buster."

"Mrs. Mackey at my school is starting up a tennis team," Mercedes volunteered. "I really want to be on it."

"I've been kind of helping her," I said, realizing I'd been left out of this conversation so far. "We try to practice on Sunday mornings."

"Really?" Rocky asked. "Where do you play?"

"Usually at Southside Park," Mercedes said. "Sometimes at City College, but the courts there are always so busy."

"Listen," Rocky said, "maybe I could meet you guys sometime. Are you going next Sunday?"

Mercedes and I looked at each other. "Sure," we answered in unison, and we all laughed.

"About nine, then? Next Sunday? Southside Park?" Rocky asked.

"Perfect," I said. "We'll be there."

Mercedes grinned broadly and dug into the pocket of her jeans. "Well, I guess I'll have a small root beer, then."

"Sorry, they don't have small root beers here, kiddo," I said.

Rocky and I just looked at each other and smiled.

I went over to Regal Oaks Manor with Mom to drop off Grandpa B's clean laundry, and he was there in his apartment entertaining the Widow Burgess. Mrs. Burgess wears a diamond-studded pince-nez on her white powdered face and is the most racially prejudiced person I have ever met. She herself comes from an "impeccable" stock of English blue bloods descended directly from William the Conqueror, or so she claims.

A baseball game was on the television, and Mrs. Burgess made such a cruel and inane comment about the ancestry of one of the players that it just left me standing there with my mouth open. The fact that she said it in that phony refined accent of hers made me want to go over and pop her one. But I respected my elders and didn't even say a word. What a coward.

After she left, Mom had a fight with Grandpa B, which really typifies the kind of person he is. It was about money. For some reason, he's always kept a wad of twenty-dollar bills in the pocket of his bathrobe, of all places (rolled up and held together with a green rubber band). Well, after Mom hung his clean robe in his closet, he stood there with his hand out, blocking her way, and said, "Where's the dough?"

Mom said, "What dough?" And then Grandpa B called her a "stupid, careless woman." Mom kept her temper and just said calmly and firmly, "There wasn't anything in any of your pockets, Dad. I've been washing clothes long enough now, I think, to remember to check the pockets."

Well, as we were leaving, my mom noticed the wad of money lying on the shelf next to his cigarettes. "So what's this?" she asked, holding it up.

Grandpa B went over and snatched it out of her hand without even apologizing. I remarked about that on the way home, and she said, "So what's new? The old coot has never apologized for anything in his entire life."

There's a small private airport nearby, and every time a plane flies low over our house, Bribe just about goes nuts, barking like a maniac and trying to catch it. He tears around the yard in a frenzy, leaping four feet in the air like a circus dog. Even Mom thinks it's cute, laughing and saying, "Look at that crazy mutt!" Could it be that Mom is changing her attitude about dogs?

Mercedes and I were out at the Southside Park courts by eight-thirty on Sunday morning. The sun was shining and there was no wind at all. Everything was perfect.

"What's going to happen when he gets here?" Mercedes asked.

"What do you mean?"

"Well, I mean are just you guys going to play, and I'm going to sit around and watch? That's what I mean."

"Of course not. Why would you say that?"

"Oh, I'm not dumb, you know. The only reason he suggested coming at all was to see you."

"Oh, Mercedes! That's not true," I said.

"Oh, Mercedes! That's not true," she mocked in a high, funny voice. "Well, anyway, I want you to promise that I'll at least get to play a little . . ."

"Hey, look!" I said suddenly. "There he is."

We both watched as Rocky drove up in a little white VW and parked under the big banyan tree on the other side of the courts. He rolled up the car window, reached in the backseat for his racket and a bucket of balls, and got out of the car. He was wearing a green and white tennis shirt and white shorts. He looked beautiful.

Mercedes needn't have worried, because it was immediately obvious that his first concern was to help her with her game. First, he checked her grip (giving her a few suggestions), and then he began tossing balls to her, asking her to show him first her forehand and then her backhand. After that he put her up next to the net and checked her volleys. At first I was sort of hovering around on the court, but then I could see I was only in the way, so I went and sat down on the wooden platform between the two courts. There was no doubt about it, Rocky was good. I could tell right away he knew what he was talking about.

After about forty-five minutes of checking out

her strokes, he started gathering up all the balls. Mercedes ran around and got all the far ones and tossed them in his bucket. When the balls were all collected, he smiled at her and said, "Okay, Sport, want to try a real game? I'll give you a three-point-per-game handicap."

She lied on the second point. (Mercedes is extremely competitive.) "Out!" she shouted, when his expert lob landed two inches inside the line.

"Mercedes!" I hollered. "That wasn't out!"

I looked across the court at Rocky. He was just standing on his baseline, staring at the ground, thoughtfully stroking his chin with his left hand and gently swinging his racket back and forth with his right.

"Come on!" Mercedes called to him. "What's wrong?"

"That was out?" he asked, his voice just loud enough to carry across the net.

Mercedes extended her hands like a fisherman describing the one that got away. "That much!" she said firmly.

"Mercedes . . ." I started, but Rocky looked at me and held up his hand, as if to say, I'll handle this. After a minute he motioned to her with his racket and started walking toward a shady spot against the back fence of the deserted courts. I decided to go over there, too.

Rocky sat down on the cool pavement and indicated that Mercedes should sit beside him. (He just ignored me, so I sat down a little ways away from both of them.) With his arms resting on his knees, he started idly bouncing a ball between his legs with the palm of his hand. He didn't say anything at first, and Mercedes just sat there watching him. She was acting a little nervous though, jiggling her foot rhythmically against her racket.

Finally, Rocky reached his fingers through the chain link fence and picked up a small stone from the ground on the other side. He spread his legs even wider and scratched a tiny X on the pavement with the rock. "This is us," he said quietly. "You and me, here on the court." He drew a small circle around the X. "This is California—the USA, and" —he drew a larger circle now, encompassing the first—". . . the Earth."

He looked sideways at her, hardly moving his head at all. I could tell he was waiting for some sort of acknowledgment from her.

"Okay." She shrugged.

He pointed a little ways off, over by the cypress trees. "The sun's over there." Then he spread his arms wide, as if he were about to embrace the entire courts. "Our solar system, the Milky Way galaxy, the universe, all spread out, all around us." He nodded at her, raising her eyebrows questioningly. "Do you see what I mean?"

"Well, I guess so," Mercedes answered. "What about it?"

Rocky cleared his throat, and looked around in a kind of conspiratorial way, as if he were checking for possible eavesdroppers. Seeing none (the three of us were alone on the courts), he continued, "Well, Sport, I have this—this *theory*. I've had it for a long time. It's, well, it's about truth." He paused. "You know the kind of truth I mean? Total, boundless, and eternal *truth*."

Mercedes stopped jiggling her foot. I leaned forward a little so I wouldn't miss a word.

"I don't talk about it much," he was saying, "because it's just one of those whimsical, crackpot ideas that seem to grab hold of you sometimes, and won't ever let you free." He was touching her arm from time to time, making sure she was paying attention.

"This whole universe, Sport, it has a certain *hum*. It *hums*, you see, in a beautiful, mystical harmony." He lowered his chin and held his body perfectly still, and in a few seconds this low, tremulous hum came from somewhere deep in his chest. He held it until he was completely out of breath. I could feel little prickles on the back of my neck, ending in a fleeting shiver. I didn't know what to think. I just kept watching and listening, and wondering what was coming next.

"The universe thrives on truth," he said. "Its strength is truth. Hey, the universe *is* truth." He paused, letting that sink in. Then he started up again. "So what happens when we lie?" he asked. "What happens when we tell a little spoken lie— like your line call—or commit a larger kind of falsehood, like when we are not true to ourselves, for instance?"

Mercedes look at him suspiciously. "I don't know. What happens?"

"The universe howls," he said simply. "It makes

a discordant howl. If there are enough lies, the friction will surely bring it to a grinding halt."

Mercedes was nodding slowly. "Oh," she said. "Oh."

"So, I guess the important thing is always remember that *nothing* that happens here on Earth is important enough to lie about. That hum—that symbolic hum—we want to keep it in perfect harmony."

Neither one of them spoke for several minutes. Rocky started bouncing the ball between his legs again. Finally, Mercedes broke the silence. "Okay, Rocky." She sighed. "You're right. The ball was in. The ball was *in*, for God's sake!"

He stood up and lightly bounced his racket off the top of his head. "Good. You can hear it, then. You can hear the music of the spheres."

Rocky stepped over to where I was sitting and stretched out his hand to me. I let him pull me up, and the three of us walked back to the court. There was no doubt about it now; for the first time in my life, I knew how it felt to be in love.

7

Something had been bothering me for quite some time, and after our session on the tennis court I finally decided to do something about it. I wrote a postcard (anonymously) to the film company that was sponsoring the Disney World photo contest (for pictures taken outside the continental USA). I told them I objected to Rule 7 of their contest—the one that stated the pictures had to be taken within the last year—and thought they should change it. "It's not fair," I wrote. "Some people can afford to go out of the country every year, and that's fine. But lots of them can't. So the rule is not fair, and it doesn't make any sense." After I mailed the post-card, I was feeling pretty good about it, until I had another thought: Some people can't *ever* afford to go out of the country. What about them?

Grandpa B came over on Saturday to fix a broken railing on our front porch. Afterward, he suggested we take Bribe to the river and see how he likes the water. My grandfather wanted to put my dog in the back of his truck for the ride over, but I said, "Nothing doing!" Instead, Bribe and I both rode up in the cab with him.

When we got there, I tied a long piece of nylon rope to the end of his regular leash, because I didn't want to risk his running away.

Grandpa B was right; Bribe loved the water. We threw a tennis ball out for him to retrieve, and he just swam over to it like a real pro. It kind of hurt my feelings, though, because it seemed that when Grandpa B yelled at him and ordered him to "Come!" Bribe would lower his head and look up at Grandpa B for a second and then run right over to him. He never does mind *me* like that. Maybe he just likes men better.

I think Grandpa B had an even better time than Bribe. He was acting like a kid, throwing that tennis ball, and a stick he had found on the beach. In fact, I'm the one who had to suggest when it was time to go home. Grandpa B sort of announced maybe he'd bring Bribe by himself someday (his way of asking my permission). At first I was going to say no, but Bribe was having such a great time, I changed my mind and said, "Well, if you do, you'd better not put him in the back of the truck."

On the way home, Bribe was so pooped he slept all the way, sprawled all over me. I told Grandpa B about the great dog park I saw in Berkeley. He just snorted and said, "Jesus, wouldn't you know. Only in Berkeley." Then he spit out the window.

* * *

The last day of school before summer vacation finally arrived. Except for one really nice thing that happened, it was a complete waste of time. I've never been able to figure out why we have to go to school that last day before summer. The grades are all in, and all we do is watch movies we've already seen and throw things at each other. We couldn't even use the time to sign each other's yearbooks, since somebody fouled up at the printing plant, and the books were going to be late again, just like last year. When that announcement came over the intercom during first period, the kids let out a real roar, and groused and groaned for the rest of the period.

The nice thing that happened was that Rocky stopped by my locker while I was cleaning it out and handed me something. It was a red-and-white bracelet that he had made out of a Styrofoam cup and pieces of red plastic coffee stir-sticks, held together, he said, with the stuff they use to repair the grout around the sink. It's really intricate and clever, and it must have taken him hours to make.

"I did it at work," he said. "I made the customers wait. Some of them got *pretty* upset," he added.

"Oh, really?" I said, trying my best not to overreact. I hate girls who gush all over the place, so I'm sure Rocky does, too.

"It's . . . it's amazing, Rocky. Truly one-of-a-kind," I said, acting like I was just humoring him, the way you'd do with a four-year-old child, for instance. Then I slipped my hand through the bracelet and gave it a twirl, as though it were just a cheap little homemade thing I might keep for a day and then carelessly toss away. (But I knew in my heart I would keep it forever.)

"Think so?" He smiled. "Truly one-of-a-kind, huh? I made it out of our *large* size cup. Could you tell?"

"Be still my heart," I said, with a teasing half-smile (open to interpretation). Rocky's eyes met mine for just an instant, but he blushed and dropped his gaze, and I didn't get the prolonged eye contact that I wanted at this stage of the game. I knew then that if our relationship was destined to develop into a real romance, it would take time for it to blossom and grow. Obviously, Rocky was going to take it very slow and easy.

It was Uncle Larry's birthday (forty-seventh) so my mother invited him and Grandpa B over for dinner. She made lasagna (Uncle Larry's favorite) with tossed green salad and hot garlic bread. Grandpa B brought Mrs. Burgess along. (Oh, he phoned Mom at the last minute, but there was no way she could refuse.)

Uncle Larry's kind of a weird guy, but lovable. He's so incredibly naive about everything, and yet he has somehow managed to make oodles of money in the real estate business. I guess his complete and guileless honesty just comes across to all of his clients. Mom told me he was so devastated by an unfortunate love affair many years ago that he gave up on women and spent all of his time and energy after that building up his business.

He and Mrs. Burgess were seated next to each other at dinner and got into a conversation about gingivitis and other gum diseases, and how more people lose their teeth because of that than on account of cavities. Mrs. Burgess said she still had all of her original teeth, knock on wood, and that she makes it a point to floss after every meal. Then the topic changed to methods of fricasseeing chicken, and, finally, to the Ku Klux Klan. When Mrs. Burgess lowered her voice and mentioned to Uncle Larry that a distant cousin of hers was some kind of "wizard" in that organization, I couldn't help myself. I interrupted her loudly and said, "In the Ku Klux Klan? Why, that's terrible!" She just sniffed and moved her shoulders around slightly and said something like, "You young people shouldn't speak about things you know nothing about." I think Mercedes was about to jump into the fray then, but Mom raised her hand and shook her head, silently cautioning her to keep quiet. I noticed my father was watching us all in his amused way, his lower jaw moving from side to side and the tips of his fingers playing around his chin.

After dinner Mom brought out the same kind of cake she's been making for Uncle Larry's birthday for years, a chocolate monstrosity she concocts with two cake mixes, a ton of whipped cream, a half pound of walnuts, and about a dozen melted chocolate bars. Uncle Larry expressed his usual amazement, and there was no doubt that he was sincere.

"Blow out the candle, Larry, and make a wish," Mom said.

"How about Europe *this* summer!" Mercedes suggested, and we all laughed gently. Uncle Larry has been talking about going to Europe for the last ten years. He's got a whole file drawer full of brochures and literature from tourist bureaus around the world, but he just can't seem to summon up the courage to pack up and go. My mom keeps telling him he should just go with a tour group, but he says he certainly doesn't want to be trapped on a bus with a gaggle of middle-aged school teachers all looking for a husband. He says he wants to see the *real* Europe, just bumming around like a college kid.

Good old Uncle Larry adjusted his glasses and brushed back his thinning blond hair. Then he pressed his lips together, took a deep breath, and blew out the candle. His eyes were watering slightly and he said, as he does each year, "Yes, I think this is the year I'm really going to do it."

"We hope so," Mercedes said, and we all nodded and smiled at each other across the table, but it was sad, all the same.

Aunt Lucille called up all excited and said she had lost twelve pounds. She really sounded good. She said she has that powdered stuff you mix with milk for breakfast and lunch, and then only eats a little bit of her regular dinner. She laughed and said it was amazing how the mere thought of her ex-mother-in-law getting the five hundred dollars really spoils her appetite.

After she hung up, something occurred to me that really left me with a funny, mysterious sense of wonder: If some unknown person had not taken my regular table at bingo that night, I wouldn't even have seen the article about the Blackmail Diet in the newspaper, and Aunt Lucille probably would still be feeling miserable and depressed.

I started my summer job. For three weeks I go to the "Mother Hutch" (that's what Mr. Bunney calls his first little store in the Thrifty parking lot), and then I go to the one on Rand Avenue. After that, they'll tell me where to go.

All I do is sell newspapers (they have the largest collection of out-of-town newspapers in the city, Mr. Bunney told me) and I also supervise the copy machine. For the newspapers, I have to consult the price list, since they're all higher than the price printed on the paper. Technically, the copy machine is supposed to be self-service, but I could tell right away that, with some people, it's a lot easier just to do it for them rather than try to explain step-by-step how to do it.

I hadn't used a copier for quite a long time before I started, and I was surprised at just how good those machines are now. The job is not that easy, though, because some of the customers are pretty rude. Like if someone is running off their stuff, people will barge in and say they "only have three or four" copies to make—and wave some papers around in the air to prove it—and they want the person who's running the machine to stop right in the middle and let them have their turn. Usually, though, instead of three or four copies, it turns out they have about fifty, and then they want colored paper and all kinds of extra stuff like that. Mr. Bunney himself trained me, and he said the best way to deal with that problem is to simply say, "first come, first served," no matter how many copies anybody says they have. He said if the line is really long, I could suggest that they do some other shopping and come back later. I thought that his slogan (Copies Kwik as a Bunney) wasn't really true then, but I didn't tell him that. He probably meant it just to be cute, anyway, and not to be taken literally.

The doorbell rang on Friday night just as we were getting ready to eat, and before anyone could get to the door, it burst open and there was Heather standing with her key in her hand. She laughed and said, "Surprise!" Allan was with her, but the funny thing was, he had his head covered with a big brown bag from Safeway. (I recognized his sandals.) Heather was leading him by the hand, and they were laughing like a couple of maniacs. My mom and dad got up from the table and were walking toward them when Heather suddenly snatched the paper bag up and said, "Parents, this is Allan! We got the green light from Dr. Gabriel! We'll be married on the Fourth!" Allan tried to smooth back that gorgeous hair with his left hand while he reached out his right one to shake hands with my dad. "Hi, Parents!" he said, as my mother and father gaped at him in amazement, and I thought to myself. *Oh, brother! Now what? Help, somebody!*

Heather explained how they were in town for two reasons. One was so that Allan could meet the family ("Hey, Mom," she said, "how about inviting everyone for dinner tomorrow night?"), and the other reason was that the next day, some splinter group from the Friends of the Earth was planning a demonstration at the chemical plant way out on Ranch Road, and Allan had written a special song for the event called "Chemical Wastes in the Lake Are Bad for the Ducks." He said the tune was pretty well fixed in his head, but he was having a bit of trouble with the words in the last verse. "Say," he asked brightly, "do any of you guys know a good rhyme for 'scummy?' "

Mercedes was really funny. She bowed her head and knit her brows and looked at him with this exaggeratedly serious expression on her face and said, "How about 'dummy?' " Then she turned to me, hiding her face from the others, and gave me the biggest, innocent-looking, mugging smirk you ever saw.

Dad and Mercedes and I had planned to start work on the dining room that weekend, but Heather's unexpected arrival put a crimp in those plans. Instead, Mom got on the phone and called Uncle Larry and Grandpa B and my other grandparents and Aunt Lucille and said, "Guess what? Heather's beau is in town! We'd love to have you come for dinner tomorrow night and meet him." Then, the next morning, instead of taking down the old dining room curtains and washing the walls so Dad could paint them, I went to the store for Mom and bought a huge ham, more than enough for twelve people. (We knew from experience that Grandpa B would bring along "that Burgess woman," as Mom called her. As if it weren't enough that she was a pro-Ku Klux Klanner and an insufferable snob, we all suspected she was after Grandpa B's money.)

Heather, Allan, and Mercedes were still at the house when I got home from the store with the ham. "Hey," I said, setting the groceries down on the kitchen counter. "What are you guys still doing here? I thought you were going out to that chemical plant to demonstrate this morning." (I was surprised that Mercedes had agreed to go with them, but she told me privately that she really supported lots of the environmental things "cuckoo Allan" said he stood for—it was just *him* she had a problem with.)

"Nah," Allan said, in answer to my question. "It's been called off." He was sitting at the table with his bare feet in Heather's lap, chewing on a matchstick.

"A guy we know phoned a little while ago," Heather explained. "He said that the chemical plant officials had finally sat down with some representatives of the Friends of the Earth, and an agreement was reached, so Slim and the others in the splinter group called off the demonstration."

"Hey, that's great!" I said.

Allan only grunted and removed his feet from Heather's lap and put them on the floor, spitting the matchstick out in little pieces into the palm of his hand.

"Well, what's wrong?" I asked him. "That *is* good news, isn't it?"

"Hell, no!" he said. "It sure as hell *ain't* good news! Now how are they going to hear my new song? Just tell me that, huh?" He pounded his fist on the table and then cradled his head in his arms.

I glanced at Mercedes. She put her hand up to her face, hiding it from Heather, and mouthed one of her favorite words to me: *Bizarre!*

But I guess this time even Heather realized he sounded childish and hypocritical, because she tousled up his hair and got this sympathetic look on her face and, pointing to our morning paper lying there on the table, said softly, "Well now, honey, remember what the Jeane Dixon column said— 'expect a setback . . .' "

He lifted his head and glared at her. "But we didn't see 'Stargazing with Gabe' today, did we? We didn't see our *personal* forecast!"

Mercedes whispered something like, "Can you believe it?" while Heather shrugged helplessly, explaining that Dr. Gabe's column is only printed in the *Berkeley Bugle*, the paper they got at home.

There were twelve of us at the dinner table that night. Grandpa B brought Mrs. Burgess along, just as we suspected he would. She was wearing a long-sleeved white cotton dress with huge cuffs and green lace around the neck. When Aunt Lucille politely complimented her on it, she said it was just a cheap little thing she purchased the last time she was in Bermuda, and she was going to give it to the Goodwill one of these days very soon.

Allan Allen was in a peculiar mood, even for Allan. He was very quiet at the beginning of dinner, and, consequently, made an excellent first impression on all the relatives. Too bad he had to open his mouth and spoil it. For a while, there was some general conversation, and then, during a slight lull, Allan suddenly broke in with a question for Mom. It was more like a demand, really. "Are there any preservatives in this ham?"

I looked at Mom and she looked back at me. "Well . . . well, uh," she stammered, "I'm not sure, Allan."

"Do you know what preservatives do to your guts?"

"Oh, *Al*lan," Heather began. "Come on, sweetheart. You *prom*ised me you wouldn't start on that tonight."

"But why do people insist on polluting their bodies?" He wiped his hands on his napkin and threw it on the table, shaking his head as if to say he just couldn't fathom the reason for such behavior.

"Take it easy, honey," Heather whispered, touching him on the arm.

That only seemed to make things worse. "The whole stinking world is polluted!" he said loudly. "Can't you people see that? And now you're eating polluted ham!"

Mercedes stifled a nervous giggle. Everyone had stopped eating, and we were stealing little sideways glances at each other. Uncle Larry cleared his throat, and Aunt Lucille coughed delicately, putting her napkin up to her mouth.

"I'm trying to tell you something," Allan said, his voice rising with barely controlled hysteria. "If only there was some way to make you all understand!"

"Allan is very sensitive about this issue," Heather started to explain. "Like all Leos, he—"

"If there was only some way I could get your attention," Allan interrupted. His glance circled the table. You could have heard a pin. "I could wreck this room, you know," he said in a tone of voice that gave me the chills. "I could go out of control and really wreck this place. That might do it. If I went out of control and wrecked the room, I wager you'd pay attention then!" He gestured toward the bowl of mashed potatoes. "I could throw food all over the walls. I could—"

"But you won't," Heather said nervously. I saw her fingers shaking as she laughed hollowly and pushed her hair back. "Sometimes, when Allan gets really frustrated with the stupidity around him, he threatens to wreck the room," she said, looking around frantically.

Allan suddenly seemed to relax just as quickly as he had become agitated a few minutes before. The crisis, apparently, was over. "Well, I could do it," he said, matter-of-factly. "I could make a shambles of this place."

No one dared to speak. Finally, Mercedes put her fork down deliberately and said in a quiet voice, "Let me get this straight, Allan. You're actually bragging that you could go out of control and wreck this room? You're actually *bragging* that you have no self-control?"

Allan grinned and shrugged one shoulder. "I guess so. Sure."

Mercedes picked up her fork again and looked directly at her plate. "That is really nuts, you know that?"

Allan leaned back, obviously pondering her remark. Then he said in a slow and patient manner, "I'm only saying that somehow there is something in my Leo makeup that gives me the ability to do something that nobody else would dare to do, that's all."

"Who said nobody else would dare to do it?" I challenged.

"Well, you won't," he said with a supercilious smile. "I could, but you couldn't."

That did it. That was just too much for me. The new curtain material was on the shelf in the closet and the paint was out in the garage. It was a once-in-a-lifetime opportunity that I couldn't pass up. Slowly and deliberately, I stood up and reached across the table to the bowl of mashed potatoes. I scooped up a huge handful and dipped it in the gravy boat. I looked first at Mercedes and then at my mother and father. Then I took a step back from the table and flung the mashed potatoes across the room, aiming at the wall directly opposite to where Allan was sitting. They hit with a beautiful thud, splattering the wall all the way to the window. Then I sat back down and, in the stunned silence that followed, said to Mercedes, "Will you please pass the gelatin salad, Sis?"

She passed it to me, eyes twinkling.

"Would anyone care for some more gelatin salad?" I asked, as I loosened it from the sides of the bowl. (It was what my dad jokingly called "The Green Death"—lime gelatin mixed with cottage cheese, walnuts, and pineapple.) "No? How about you, Mercedes?" and saying that, I held the bowl out to her across the table. She quickly reached in with both hands (bless her heart), whirled around, and whopped the other wall. My mom, who had drunk two glasses of wine before dinner, now got into the act. She grabbed a handful of peas from the bowl and, laughing, flung them at Mercedes like so much confetti. Mercedes retaliated by whopping a handful of gelatin salad right at Mom. Half of it missed, some landing on the purple curtains and some on poor Mrs. Burgess.

I guess the best way to describe the next couple of minutes would be to call it utter pandemonium. Allan Allen appeared to be absolutely flabbergasted, and it was a pale and stunned Mrs. Burgess who rose regally from the table and announced that she had never witnessed anything so utterly vulgar in her entire life, and she wished to be taken home immediately. The cuffs of the white dress she had purchased in Bermuda were full of peas, and we heard her say to Grandpa B on their way out that she was definitely going to reevaluate their relationship in light of this disgraceful exhibition. As soon as the door closed behind them we all yelled, "Hurrah!"

Except for Allan Allen, that is. He was just sitting at the table, scratching his head and staring at the purple drapes, which were lying in a heap on the floor. (In a particularly dramatic moment, Mom had really gotten into the spirit of things and just jerked them off their hooks and jumped up and down all over them.)

Allan had acted like such an egotistical fool with his bragging little speech about his "Leo makeup," I just couldn't resist taunting him about it. "Hey, Allan," I said, stepping over the drapes and finger painting a huge letter A on the wall with a gob of mashed potatoes and gravy. "Not a bad show for a simple little Aquarius, wouldn't you say?"

After everyone went home that night I had a short talk with Mercedes, which almost ended in a fight. It was about Heather, of course.

"We *have* to do something," I said. "We can't let her marry Allan, and that's all there is to it."

"Who are you?" Mercedes asked, looking down at her hands and clicking her thumbnails nervously. "Who are you?" she repeated. "God?"

"What are you *talking* about?" I answered angrily. "You saw how he was tonight! He's really nuts, Mercedes! You even said so yourself!"

Mercedes just sighed and didn't answer. It was maddening.

"So you just want to sit back and watch her self-destruct? Is that it?"

"She knows how we feel, Cairo," Mercedes said evenly. "Now it's up to her. We can't tie her up and put her in the basement, you know."

"No, but we can do *something!*"

"What? What can we do? Don't you see? She *knows* how we feel! My God, don't you remember how she blew up when I told her I didn't think she should marry him?"

"Yes, but—"

"At some point, we have to butt *out!* I hate to say it, but Heather has to be free to make her own mistakes."

"I can't believe you'd actually say that," I said. "And you're supposed to be the smart one!"

"Just what is that supposed to mean?"

"It means that for being the smart one, you seem awfully dumb to me!"

"You know, Cairo," she said evenly, "your trouble is that you think you have a right to interfere in everyone's business—"

"I can't believe you're saying that!" I interrupted. "I thought you'd be the first to agree with me! I thought you'd help me think of a way to—"

"Well, you were wrong!" she said loudly. "And while you're at it, maybe you'd better read the Constitution!"

"Well, you self-righteous little twit! You little miss know-it-all!"

"That's right!" she shouted. "Get personal!"

Suddenly the door opened and there stood Mom

in her bathrobe. "Would you girls *mind?*" she asked, shutting her eyes and putting her hand to her forehead. "My head is killing me."

Mercedes got up and flounced out of the room, looking at me crossly over her shoulder as she went.

I knew then that if anyone was going to save Heather, it was going to have to be me. And I didn't have the foggiest notion of how I was going to do it.

8

My cousin Margaret called up from San Francisco and added more fuel to the fire. She said she was in Berkeley on business again and dropped in at Frog-pond. She found Heather with a bruise the size of a golf ball on her face. Margaret said she finally wormed it out of her that Allan did it. He happened to have a stapler in his hand and went a little ber-serk. "Heather tried to cover up for him," Margaret said, "by saying he really didn't mean to hurt her. Heather told me she just 'got in the way' of the stapler, that's all."

I almost told Mercedes about it, thinking maybe that would change her mind about "interfering in Heather's life," as she called it, but then I figured the first thing she'd do would be to go ahead and tell Mom. Then Mom would try to take charge and *forbid* Heather to marry him, which, knowing Heather, would immediately send her off eloping to Reno in a taxicab. So I just kept it to myself, worrying in solitude about what I should do now. All the while I was hoping (unrealistically) that

Heather herself would change her mind, even though I knew the chances of that were almost zero. After all, according to Heather, it was in the stars.

And then a strange thing happened: I accidentally found out that Grandpa B had to go to Berkeley Thursday afternoon on lodge business. (It was purely accidental that I found out, because I left my shoes in the front room, and when I went in there to get them, Mom just happened to be telling Dad about Grandpa B's plan.) Grandpa B is the Grand Esteemed Honored Illustrious High Potentate (or something like that) in his lodge, and he had to hand deliver some important Highly Secret Papers to the Supergrand Mucky-Mucks in Berkeley. I thought that would be the perfect opportunity for me to drop in on Heather and see exactly what was going on. (And while I was at it, I thought, I could take Bribe, and we could go to that dog park, too. I could use the dog park as an excuse to see Heather!) So I called up Grandpa B and asked him if that would be okay—for him to take me to the dog park, I mean. I explained to him that the park is practically right on his way, and that I might take a little walk and drop in on Heather while I was at it. He said it wouldn't cut any ice with him (whatever that means), but that he wanted to leave around one in the afternoon. Then I had to call Mr. Bunney and see if he could get this other girl, Marcia, to work for me Thursday afternoon. It was a lot of trouble setting it up, since he told me I had to call Marcia myself, and she was always "out." At least that's what her mother told me. I know she wasn't "out" every time, because the last time I called, I distinctly heard her saying, "If that's Cairo again, tell her I'm out."

I guess her mother was fed up, though, because she said, "Here, tell her yourself, Bozo."

In order for Marcia to agree to work one Thursday afternoon for me, I had to agree to work all day Saturday, my day off, for her. (Talk about Bozo!)

It was about two-thirty Thursday afternoon when Grandpa B dropped Bribe and me off at the dog park in Berkeley. He said he figured he'd be gone for about two hours, so I told him I was going to walk over to see Heather, but I'd meet him back at the park around four-thirty.

There were only two dogs in the park—a toy poodle and one of those little mop-type dogs that (according to Mercedes) looked like something you'd put on the end of a stick to wash windows with.

Bribe was kind of squealing and barking, straining to get through the gate and join the fun, but I was anxious to get over to Frogpond first, and see if I could find out anything about Heather. It took me about ten minutes to walk over there, and I was happy to see her sitting on the downstairs porch playing some kind of board game with two guys and another girl. She was sure surprised to see us. "What are you doing here?" she said, jumping down the steps. "And Bribe! Where'd you come from, anyway?"

I had decided on the way over that I wouldn't let on to Heather that Margaret had called me. "Grandpa B had some business here, so he dropped Bribe and me off at the dog park and I just thought, heck, we're so close, we'd come and see if you were home. And you are!" Then I acted real surprised and said, "Heather! What happened to your head?"

She quickly lifted her hand and covered the purple spot on her forehead. "Oh, nothing," she said. "It's better now."

I removed her hand with my own and peered at the bruise. "But what happened? Let me see. Heather! You had stitches!"

"Only three," she said, kneeling down to hug Bribe. "It's nothing, really."

"But what happened?" I persisted.

"Her boyfriend hit her with a stapler," one of the guys on the porch said loudly.

"He did *not*, Doyle!" Heather said firmly.

"Well, that's what I heard."

"You heard wrong!" Heather retorted.

"Allan did it?" I asked. "When? Where is he?"

Heather's face was red and flushed. "Allan did *not* do it, Cairo! And he's sitting a house in Danville for a couple of days. And sure, he was holding the stapler, but he didn't hit me on purpose, Cairo. See, what happened was, he had been stapling some of his music, and he . . . uh, he heard something on the television that upset him, and he whirled around like this . . ." and Heather demonstrated, turning quickly around with her right arm outstretched, ". . . and whammo, the stapler connected with my forehead, right here."

"That's not the way *I* heard it," came the singsongy voice again from the porch.

"Just shut up!" Heather said angrily. "You don't know anything." Then she turned to me. "Come on," she said, "let's get out of here. We can go for a walk. Let's walk back to the dog park."

"Well," I said, pulling on Bribe's leash, "I guess if anyone knows what happened, you should."

Heather looked up at me quickly, too quickly. "Yes!" she said. "That's right!"

When we got back to the park, there were three more dogs there, and Bribe nearly went crazy making friends with them all. He ran after a little cocker spaniel first, and they sniffed each other from head to toe, tails wagging like mad, and then he repeated the process with every other dog there. I thought his tail was going to drop off, it was wagging so hard.

Heather and I didn't talk anymore about her bruise, and she seemed relieved that we didn't. She said Doyle (the guy on the porch) was just a big troublemaker and didn't know what he was talking about.

I wanted to believe her version of what happened, but I knew her too well for that. I could always tell when Heather was not being completely honest, and this time I almost knew for certain she was lying through her teeth. (I got a sudden vision of Rocky, stopping dead in his tracks and clapping his hands over his ears to shut out the screechy dissonance of the spheres.)

I now felt I had no choice. I simply had to do *something* to prevent her from making the most terrible mistake of her life. Direct confrontation was out of the question. After witnessing her reaction to Mercedes' attempt at that, I was sure that for me to advise her against marrying him in so many words would be like holding up a red banner in front of a bull.

When Grandpa B came back to pick us up, he hung around almost an extra half hour before giving Heather a ride back to Frogpond. He was having lots of fun throwing a Frisbee to some little black-and-white mongrel who could jump about fifteen feet up in the air and twist around in a circle while he was at it. All the way home I kept raving about what a great idea dog parks were, but Grandpa B would only reply with grunts and spits.

After he dropped me off at my house, I got a terrific idea. What if I asked Grandpa B if he could give Heather a nice present—like a trip to Hawaii for a month or so, right around the Fourth of July? (*Before* her wedding, of course.) Heather has always talked about how she was dying to go there and visit that longtime pen pal of hers. We could tell her she could get married when she returned. Dr. Gabriel could easily find some "good days" in August. And maybe by that time, well, who knows? With Heather, anything could happen in a month! She might even come home married to her pen pal's brother! Well, actually, the more I thought about it, the more far-out it seemed, especially getting Grandpa B to cough up the money. But if I really put my mind to it, and figured out just the right way to broach it to him—like appealing to that maverick side of him—it just might work.

Our washing machine broke, so I went with Mom to the Laundromat. Mom didn't call the repairman because the last time they got it fixed, it cost over eighty dollars, and my dad said he was tired of throwing money down that hole. The thing is, I think I was the one who broke it. I washed Bribe's blanket, which was covered with dog hair, and I have a feeling it wrecked the filter or something. I decided to confess that to Mom at the Laundromat. I knew from experience that keeping something like that to myself, well, it would begin to bother me. I had just gotten up to check the dryer and went back to where Mom was sitting, thumbing through an old *Redbook*. It was so full of holes where people had torn out recipes and coupons that it looked like it had been used by a family of rats who were remodeling their nest.

"I might have broken the washing machine, Mom," I said. "I washed Bribe's blanket in it. I don't know, but it might have clogged up the filter or something."

Mom just nodded, and, at first, I wondered whether she had heard me right. She didn't get mad or anything. She turned a couple of pages and the magazine suddenly fell apart and spilled all over the floor.

"What the hell," she said, and I didn't know if she was talking about the washing machine or the magazine. She scooped up all the loose pages and threw them all in the garbage can, and we finished the wash and went home.

It started raining while I was at work. It was one of those freaky, soft, early summer rains that I really love, with raindrops all fat and plump and warm. It was as if someone were tossing quarters out of the dark, gray sky, and they were landing like polka dots on the pavement. No one was in the shop, so I could just look out my window and enjoy it, smelling that uniquely pleasant smell that comes up from parking lots during an unexpected summer shower like this. I don't usually spend a lot of time wondering whether I'm happy or not, but all of a sudden I was conscious of a definite feeling of unmistakable happiness.

Mom called and offered to pick me up after work. (I found out later she really wanted me to run into the cleaners and drop off some clothes for her, which I did.) On the way home, while she was stopped at a light, I saw a big German shepherd run across the street on the other side of the crosswalk. It had that same wild look of unaccustomed freedom that Bribe had when he took off down the street that time when those people returned him.

"Wait, Mom!" I said suddenly, just as she put the car in gear and started up again. "There's a lost dog!" I opened my door, fully expecting that Mom would pull over to the curb. But she didn't. She didn't even stop.

"Shut that door!" she yelled. "What a crazy thing to do!"

"But, Mom, that dog was—"

"We're not stopping for any stray dogs, Cairo," she said.

"But someone found my dog and brought him home to me!" I argued. "Now I have to do the same for someone else! I have to keep it going, don't you see?"

Mom turned and gave me such a stern, warning look, I had to stop talking. I could feel the frustration welling up in me, but I didn't even see the dog anymore, and I knew it would be useless to argue about it any longer.

That unexplained feeling of happiness I had experienced earlier had suddenly disappeared without a trace.

A lady came into the Copy Shop with a "Cathy" comic strip showing Cathy and Andrea talking about some mutual acquaintance in a kind of derogatory manner. The lady had a pair of scissors and some paper, and she carefully cut out the friend's name in the comic strip, pasted some blank paper in the hole, and wrote in the name Debbie, which was her sister's name, in the space, making it look like Cathy and Andrea were saying this bad stuff about somebody named Debbie. Then we put the whole strip in the machine and made a copy. I was amazed at how good it came out. You wouldn't suspect anyone had doctored it up at all. The lady laughed and said she was going to mail it to her sister anonymously, but of course her sister would know right away who sent it.

Rocky called me up just as my father and I were leaving to go pick up the Tuesday Night Special Half-Price Pizza at Angelo's Pizza Parlor for dinner.

"Having a nice summer?" he asked.

"Hey, school hasn't been out that long," I said, laughing. "But so far it's okay. How about you?"

"I'm working most of the time, so it's pretty boring."

"Yeah. I know what you mean."

"Cairo!" It was my dad. "Come on, let's go."

"Except for Wednesday nights, that is," Rocky was saying, and I felt my breath stop in midair and hang there for a second.

"Really?" I teased, doing my best to keep my voice steady. "And what happens on Wednesday nights that makes them so special?"

"Wednesday nights? Oh. Well, gee, that's the night we scrape the crud off the grill and spray for roaches. Yessir! Wednesday nights, things are really hopping around here."

"Hmm," I said. "I'll bet."

"Cairo!" Darn! Dad again.

"Oh, Rocky, I'm sorry, but I have to go," I said.

"Yeah. I heard someone shouting for you."

"That was my dad. So I guess . . ."

"Okay, I'll talk to you later, then. But wait! Hey, listen. Cairo?"

"Yes?"

"Ask your dad when can I see those slides? You know, their Egypt slides."

"Are you kidding? You really want to see those old things?" (*Say yes! Say yes!*)

"I'd love to see them!"

"Well, okay then. I'll ask him. I'm sure he'll say yes, though."

"Great. See you tomorrow night. And, oh," he added suddenly, "one more thing, real fast. I, uh, was just joking about the roaches."

"You were?" Heart thumping again.

"Yeah." He paused. "But not about the grill. Scraping the crud off the grill—now *that's* what I call exciting!"

"Rocky," I said. "After you scrape the crud off the grill, how about scraping the crud off your brain?"

Later, after the pizza, I told my mom and dad that Rocky wanted to see their Egypt slides.

"Rocky?" Dad asked. "Who's Rocky?"

But Mom knew who I meant. "That boy at the Snack Shack?" she asked, and I just nodded as nonchalantly as possible.

"Well," Dad said in a deep voice, rubbing his chin and pretending like he was thinking it over (they adore showing their ten million slides), "I imagine that could be arranged."

We decided Sunday evening would be best, since I knew Rocky didn't work that night. I called him after he got home and told him it was all set up for Sunday night. And I added (in a joking way) that he should tell his mother not to expect him home for at least two weeks.

I don't get a real lunch break at the Copy Shop. What I'm supposed to do is stick this little sign that Mr. Bunney made on the door. It's just a cardboard clock face with movable hands and the words

Out to Lunch. Will Return at

and I'm supposed to set the little hands. Well, it doesn't work. People see me in there eating my lunch, and it's impossible to shoo them away.

I was right in the middle of my peanut butter and chocolate chip sandwich when Mrs. Schroeder tapped at the window right by my chair. About once every six months, I run into her some place. She has a degree or credential or something like that in child psychology, and her job is to go around from school to school counseling troubled children. When I was in the fourth grade, my teacher had recommended to my parents that they avail themselves of that service and get some counseling for me. In my teacher's opinion, I was acting unusually withdrawn and depressed. The trouble was, I would look at the chalkboard and all I could see was blood and strawberries. That's when I started my appointments with Mrs. Schroeder.

I put my sandwich down on the table next to the copy machine and let Mrs. Schroeder in, locking the door after her.

"Well, what are you doing here, Cairo, dear?" she asked.

"I work here." I smiled. "It's my summer job."

"Well, that's wonderful." She opened a little briefcase and took out some music. "Got some stuff here for the children's choir. At my church, you know."

"Oh."

She knew exactly what to do. I didn't even have to remind her to turn on the machine, like I have to do to 90 percent of the general public.

"I need twenty-five copies of each," she said, pushing all the right buttons. After she got the machine started, she stepped over to me and gave me a big hug. "And so how are you doing these days?"

Sometimes, when people ask, "How are you doing?" you know they're only being polite, and they don't really give a darn how you're doing. But Mrs. Schroeder's not like that. With her, you can tell she really cares. "I'm doing fine," I said. And, as she turned to check the copy machine, fourth-grade memories came tumbling back from out of the past. Mostly, I remembered how I had just "opened up" and let it all pour out during our very first session. It happened on the day after Christmas, I told her. We were having a combination Christmas and good-bye party for my little cousin Jerry and his sister and parents. They were planning to leave the next morning for a week at an exclusive ski school in the Swiss Alps, near Lucerne. The star pupil was going to be little Jerry. (Uncle Walter had almost made the Olympic Ski Team when he was seventeen, and he was certain that if only he had learned to ski at an earlier age, he would surely have won an Olympic medal or two. So he was determined not to make the same mistake with little Jerry that his parents had made with him.) Jerry got his first pair of skis the day after he learned how to walk. The fact that he detested everything about the sport didn't seem to faze Uncle Walter one little bit. "He'll love it someday," he kept saying. "Before you know it, he'll love putting on those skis, just like his old dad." But five-year-old Jerry would only stamp his foot and lisp, "Oh, no I won't! I hate it, hate it, hate it!"

Well, all of us cousins exchanged presents under the tree that year. I gave Jerry an Etch-a-Sketch (with my parents' money, of course), and he gave me an exercise machine for my doll. That was the Christmas my parents bought the used piano for Heather, and all day long she and our cousin Dawn were banging on it together, running their thumbnails up and down the keyboard and playing chopsticks on every octave.

My mother had made a special cake, decorated with a mountain of "snow" (seven-minute frosting) and a tiny plastic skier that Mercedes found as a prize in a box of breakfast cereal. The strawberries to spoon over the cake were defrosting in a blue bowl on the sink board. It was about three in the afternoon. The brand new Christmas blender (Dad's gift to Mom) was plugged in next to the toaster. I was showing Jerry how it worked, but my mother walked into the room just as I experimentally pushed the button marked Mix.

"No, no, Cairo," Mom said. "Don't touch the new blender, please."

She lifted it and moved it to the back of the counter, on the other side of the toaster. Then she got the eggnog mix out of the refrigerator and went back to join the others. Heather and Dawn were starting another round of chopsticks.

"Hey, Cairo, can you make a milk shake in that?" Jerry asked, pointing to the blender. "A strawberry milk shake?"

All of a sudden I remembered my forecast in the morning astrology column: *You shine in the kitchen today, Waterbaby! A culinary concoction could astound them all, so go ahead and mix it up.*

"Sure," I said. "I can make a milk shake. Want to see?" I reached in the freezer and got out the ice cream. Using a tablespoon, I scooped two large hunks into the blender, first moving it back to where it was before my mother had come into the room. It had rubber feet and wouldn't slide easily. It skidded and bumped across the counter, and left little black marks on the tile. I spooned a tablespoon of partially thawed whole strawberries into the blender, over the ice cream, and pushed the Mix button on the blender just as Jerry said, "Wait!" and quickly reached his little hand in the glass container to pull out one big red strawberry that had caught his eye. Suddenly there was blood and strawberries and a child's shrill scream, and the noise from the piano abruptly stopped.

The astrology column, said Mrs. Schroeder, was the real culprit. She even wrote a letter to the editor of the newspaper, asking that the astrology column be discontinued, since it had no basis in fact, was anti-Christian, and could be harmful to the public. The newspaper boxed in her letter and featured it as "The Letter of the Week," but it kept the astrology column right where it was.

After a few deprogramming sessions, I came to agree completely with Mrs. Schroeder. The astrologer was a low-down swine who lied to me and (along with my own unfortunate disobedience) caused me a ton of grief.

Three days after Christmas, I found Jerry's Etch-a-Sketch under the couch. I gave it to my mom, and she wrapped it in newspaper, put it in a paper bag, and stuck it on the top shelf of the hallway closet. Jerry was still in the hospital, and the Spenders didn't want anything to do with the Hays family, then or forevermore.

9

The first thing I did when I got home from work (as always) was to go in the yard and call Bribe. When he didn't come, I went and checked his alcove in the garage. He wasn't there either, and that's when I first felt something might be wrong. God, I'll never forget that sick feeling of dread. I ran around by the side of the house, then, where he had escaped that other time, saying to myself, *Please, God—Please, God.* That's when Mom opened the window and put her face right up next to the screen and told me that she had some very, very bad news.

I practically had to drag the details out of her, and I was getting frantic. It was Grandpa B, she said. He was taking Bribe to the river for a swim, and he let him ride in the back of the pickup. "I told him not to do that!" I practically screamed. "So what happened, Mom? Where is my dog? Is he dead? Is he dead? *Tell* me!"

And then my mom started to cry, and I knew he was dead. My poor Bribe fell out of the truck and got run over by a lady on the freeway. My poor

Bribe was dead, and all I could think about was that soft brown fur around his neck all matted with blood.

I went to my bed and stayed there all night, just thinking about Bribe's understanding eyes that I could never look into again, and his silky golden fur that I could never pet again. Mom called me for dinner, but how could I eat? Mercedes and my dad tried to come and talk to me, but I told them to please go away. About seven-thirty that evening, the phone rang and Mom came up to me very softly and told me there was someone on the phone who wanted to talk to me about Bribe. I got a crazy idea that maybe it was the vet or somebody to tell me they only *thought* he was dead, but that he was really still alive. It wasn't that at all, of course. It was the lady who ran over him. She was terribly upset, and said she never felt so bad about anything in her life. She started to tell me that she had a dog, too, but then she started to cry. I tried to tell her it wasn't her fault, but I couldn't finish my sentence. Finally we both just hung up. I knew it wasn't her fault, but I hated her all the same.

I couldn't stand to think about Grandpa B, but I kept seeing his stupid face every time I closed my eyes. He didn't even call me, and it's a good thing he didn't, because I only would have hung up on him as soon as I heard his disgusting voice. Naturally, my idea about asking him to send Heather to Hawaii for a month went right out the window. It probably wouldn't have worked, anyway. It even sounded stupid to *me*, now.

144

Mom called Mr. Bunney for me and told him I probably wouldn't be able to come in the next day. I didn't know if she told him the reason or not. Pretty soon René came over to try to cheer me up, so then I realized Mom *did* tell him what happened. René meant well, but when she said, "You can always get another dog," I knew that she didn't understand how I felt at all. But Rocky would understand. I mean, he would understand how I felt, but he wouldn't understand the reason Bribe had to die. And I don't either. Rocky is right. The world is insane. There is no meaning or purpose to it at all.

Late that night Grandpa B finally called up and talked to Mom awhile. Then Mom came and told me that he wanted to talk to me. I wouldn't do it. "Cairo," Mom repeated, "your grandfather wishes to speak to you." I shook my head. I was starting to cry again. She could drag me to the phone, but she couldn't make me talk. Finally, she sighed and went back to the phone and made some excuse for me. I don't know what it was because I was too upset to pay any attention to what she said.

Two days later I was still feeling rotten. Rocky was supposed to come over and look at the slides the next night. I asked Mom to please call him and postpone it for a while, but she wouldn't do it. Then she and I had a talk (her idea), and she told me she knew I was really devastated, but life goes on, and all that. I guess you could call it a pep talk. With her urging, I finally made myself call Mr. Bunney and tell him I'd report for work on Monday

morning. Mom gave me an encouraging nod and
handed me the newspaper. I took it to my room and
got back into bed. I told myself I'd read the entertainment section all the way through and try not to
think about Bribe the entire time. Soon I got to the
horoscope column (which I usually make a point of
avoiding), but this time I read everyone's forecast
for the day. The last one listed was for Pisces (Feb.
19–March 20): *"Whoa! Stop everything. Recent unexpected developments call for a complete revamping of
plans. Risks are too great."*

I let the paper slide to the floor in a heap, and
suddenly, out of the blue, I found myself formu-
lating a surefire plan to scotch my sister's wedding
that was so underhanded and deceitful, I couldn't
dare reveal it to a living soul.

Uncle Larry borrows our vacuum cleaner twice
a year and vacuums the rug in his front room,
whether it needs it or not (family joke). Once Mom
asked him why on Earth didn't he get someone to
come in and clean for him, but he said he just didn't
feel right about it. "It's my dust, I can vacuum it,"
he said. Then Mom said, "Well, you can at *least*
buy your own vacuum!" And he said, "Why? I
only use it twice a year!"

As it happened, he dropped by to return it just
as Dad was putting up the screen to show the Egypt
slides for Rocky.

"Slides?" Uncle Larry asked, after he put the
vacuum in the hallway closet.

"Egypt slides," Dad said. "Have a seat."

"Egypt slides, eh?" Uncle Larry asked, winking at me. "Say, I haven't seen them for several months now, I believe." He looked over at Rocky. "Aha! A new victim, I see. Howdy. I'm Larry. Cairo's uncle."

"Oh, I'm sorry," I said. "Uncle Larry, this is Rocky. Rocky, my Uncle Larry."

"Okay, that's it," Dad broke in. "No more conversation." He motioned with his head. "Cairo . . . lights."

I got up and switched off the lights.

"Hey! Wait for me!" Mom said, coming in from the kitchen and sitting in her chair next to Dad's.

"Mercedes!" I called out. "Egypt slides! Hurry!"

"Thanks, but no thanks," came her muffled reply.

"Okay," Dad started. "Here we are at the airport—"

"I took that picture," Uncle Larry said. "Got up at six-thirty in the morning to give you a ride to—"

"Quiet!" Dad ordered. "This is my trip. I'll do the talking. After you go on *your* trip, Larry—*when* you go on your trip," he added pointedly, "then you can show *your* slides and I'll do the interrupting."

Dad only meant to be funny, but I saw Uncle Larry's face by the light of the projector, and instead of a smile, I thought I saw a disconsolate frown.

The next three hours were filled with pyramids and camels and mummies and hieroglyphics and colossi, and the special "Fly in the Croissant" three-slide production, during which Rocky stretched out his leg and gently kicked me on the foot. When the image of the little Muslim boy suddenly appeared on the screen, Rocky exclaimed, "What a great picture!" but I noticed Dad's neck stiffen, and he and I were conspicuously silent while Mom told the story that ended with "Baksheesh!"

After the slides were over, Mercedes came out of her room and we all sat around and had pie and ice cream in the front room. Uncle Larry and Rocky started talking about traveling, and—without meaning to, I know—monopolized the conversation for the next couple of hours.

It started out with Uncle Larry sitting across the room from Rocky, but after about five minutes, he got up and moved his chair right next to the couch where Rocky and I were sitting.

"A Eurailpass is really the best way to get around in Europe, I think," Rocky was saying. "You buy the pass here, before you go over there. And then you're free to just pick up and go anytime you get tired of a place."

"What about renting a car?" Uncle Larry asked.

"Way too expensive, for one person," Rocky replied. "Besides, I think it would be more fun on the train. Most European trains have those six-person compartments, you know, like in the movies, and I think that'd be a lot more interesting than just driving alone in a car. You could meet and talk to the people that way."

"Yes, but I don't speak a foreign language,"

Uncle Larry said. Then he added, "Oh, well, come to think of it, I did study French in college, but that was so long ago . . ."

"I'm sure that many Europeans speak at least a little English these days," Rocky answered. "Especially the younger people. And then, there are always those Berlitz phrase books to help you out." Uncle Larry nodded, and Rocky continued, "But, you know, from the reading I've done, I seem to get the impression that if you're friendly and want to communicate, you can find a way."

"What kind of reading have you done?" Uncle Larry asked.

Rocky shrugged in a self-deprecating sort of way. "Well, pretty much, actually. See, I like to read travel books a lot—"

"He reads *Let's Go Europe*," I said to Uncle Larry. "He told me he knows exactly where he'd stay and the first thing he'd see in every city."

"Well, I guess it's kind of like a hobby with me, reading travel books," Rocky said. "But I really *do* plan to travel abroad, someday . . ." He shrugged again, and blushed a little this time, as if he realized he had been doing most of the talking and was embarrassed about it.

"What would you see first in . . . oh, Milan, say?" Uncle Larry asked.

"Milano's a toss-up, I think," Rocky answered, giving the Italian pronunciation without even a trace of self-consciousness. "There's Da Vinci's *Last Supper* and La Scala, the great opera house, but the Duomo there is world famous." He grinned. "I

149

have a jigsaw puzzle of the Duomo that I worked when I was about ten years old. I remember I wanted to see it even way back then."

"So?" Uncle Larry prodded. "Which would you see first?"

"When you come right down to it, I'd probably check out the Duomo first."

I couldn't stand it any longer. "What's the *Duomo*, anyway?"

Uncle Larry looked at me in amazement. "The big church, Cairo. A duomo is a big church—like a cathedral." He had been sitting there in rapt attention, leaning forward in his chair. But now he settled back again and sighed deeply, looking directly at Rocky. "I want to go to Europe, too. Someday." He shook his head. "But I just don't think I could manage on my own."

"Oh, sure you could!" Rocky said, a picture of confidence. "What is there to manage?"

Uncle Larry shook his head again. "Well, what about that foreign money, for example. Where do you exchange it, and how do you know the currency rates, and things like that?"

"Well, you shop around, of course," Rocky said. "Usually, though, the best rates are given in the banks. Train stations and airports are a little higher. But then, you have to consider banking hours. In Europe, the banks are generally open during weekdays for a couple of hours in the morning. The larger ones may open again in the afternoons for a while."

"You *are* a font of information, aren't you?"

Uncle Larry said. "You know, you'd make an excellent traveling companion for a more retiring sort like me."

"Anytime you're ready," Rocky said jokingly, "as long as you pay my way."

Everyone laughed except Uncle Larry.

That went on until almost two in the morning, and my dad practically had to chase them out of the house. Rocky lingered for a few minutes, talking quietly to me on the porch, thanking me for inviting him, and raving about what a "neat guy" Uncle Larry was.

"Hey, listen, Rocky," I said, suddenly getting a great idea. "Why don't you come to Cloverdale Circle's Fourth of July Block Party? Uncle Larry will be there, and—"

"Oh, sure!" he said. "I'd really like that!"

"And your mom! Bring your mom, too." I paused and added, "Uncle Larry will bring the potato chips." Then I laughed. Rocky looked puzzled, of course, so I started to explain about Uncle Larry and the potato chips. I didn't get very far, though. It was like, all of a sudden I realized, what was I *doing* there, laughing and having fun? I had completely forgotten about Bribe!

I couldn't stop the tears from welling up in my eyes. I turned away from Rocky, but the more I tried not to cry, the worse it became. I felt so guilty and miserable. *Oh, my poor Bribe!*

"Cairo," Rocky said, touching my arm and bringing his face close to mine. "Cairo! You're crying! What's wrong? My gosh, what did I do?"

"Oh, no, Rocky," I managed to say. "It's not you! It's just that, see, my dog got run over . . ." I couldn't say any more.

Rocky took me in his arms then and gently pressed my head against his shoulder. He reached in his back pocket and pulled out a large white handkerchief and handed it to me. "I know about that," he said quietly. "Your mother took me aside tonight and told me about it. I'm really sorry, Cairo. I know how awful you must feel."

He stood there holding me for a few minutes while I wiped my eyes and blew my nose. Then I tried to hand him the handkerchief back, but he just wrapped my fingers around it and shook his head. "You keep it," he said. The next thing I knew, we were kissing. I didn't understand how I could be both so sad and so happy at the very same time.

Mercedes was having a lazy summer, tinkering around trying to get ideas for the Fall Science Follies, the theme of which is "Original Games." I told her that sounded like an odd theme to me, but she said the games have to demonstrate scientific principles. Her latest effort, while difficult to describe, is truly spectacular. It's a "game" made out of Popsicle sticks, dominoes, and marbles. The base of it is a large piece of plywood that Heather used to work her jigsaw puzzles on. First, Mercedes nailed a long piece of wood about one inch thick under the top edge of the board, so the whole thing is on a slight slant. Then she got busy and glued the Popsicle sticks onto the plywood, making little haphazard barriers all over the board. The dominoes (about fifty or so) are placed on the little marked-off areas, standing on the edges. Some of the dominoes have different colored marbles of varying sizes resting in front of them.

Now this is how it works: You start a marble rolling from anywhere on the top raised edge of the board. This marble rolls down like in a pinball machine, and soon topples over a domino. If that domino is holding back a marble, it releases it. Then that second marble, in turn, runs down the board and maybe knocks over another domino, which releases another marble, and so forth and so on. In the meantime, the first marble is still making its way down, perhaps knocking down more dominoes, perhaps not. Eventually, all the marbles that were released end up dead in a trough at the bottom edge of the board, leaving behind a trail of prone and scattered dominoes. The amazing thing about it is that the pattern never seems to repeat itself. The board looks different at the end of each "roll."

The only trouble is, even though it's fascinating to watch and lots of fun to play around with, it doesn't have a name, and there doesn't seem to be any real point to it at all.

Grandpa B paid a stupid surprise visit while I was home. I had been dreading seeing him, so when I heard his truck in the driveway, I went right to my room and locked the door. I was sure my mother would force me to come out, but, miraculously, she let me be. I could hear them talking in the other room, but they didn't say anything about Bribe. There were talking about Mrs. Burgess, who is now keeping constant company with a gentleman named Conrad Longstreet, who lives on the second floor at Regal Oaks Manor. Grandpa B laughed and said it was about time he got rid of "that dizzy broad." The sound of his laugh made me sick to my stomach. I didn't know I could actually hate anyone so much.

After he left, I came out of my room, and Mom ignored me while I watched TV awhile. When I started setting the table, she handed me the napkins and told me that she had heard from Aunt Ginger again. Their plans are definite now, Mom said. They'll leave Phoenix tomorrow, spend a few days with a college friend of Ginger's in Los Angeles, and arrive in town on the first of July. They've got reservations at the Holiday Inn and will call us when they arrive. They are so happy that Heather took steps to end this long estrangement, and they are all looking forward to her happy wedding day, especially Dawn, who (Mom continued) is engaged now to a fine young man herself.

I've been reading the "Stargazing with Gabe" column in the *Berkeley Bugle* every day at work, and at last I've found the perfect forecast—exactly what I have been looking for in order to implement my plan for Heather's future. It was Tuesday's advice to Taurus (April 20–May 20): *"Cancel all plans for* tomorrow. *You may be on the verge of making a monumental mistake, stemming from a misinterpretation of signs and signals of a former time. Have courage, and follow your deepest instincts.*"

I bought two copies of the *Bugle* (just to be safe), and clipped out the astrology columns from both papers. A customer walked in just then, and I quickly slipped the clippings into a folder and shoved them into the drawer of my desk. I felt like a thief, even though I knew I paid for the papers and they were mine to do with as I wished. What was wrong with me, anyway?

When I got home, there was a big bouquet of flowers on the hall table. I was surprised to see my name on the pink envelope. Thoughts of Rocky jumped into my head as I tore open the envelope and pulled out the card. But it was from Aunt Lucille. I had never seen so many exclamation points in one little note before: "I have lost another ten (10!) pounds!!" she wrote. "That completes my contract with you way before the deadline!! So let's consider it *renewed* as of today! Same terms as before! NOTHING CAN STOP ME NOW!!! Thank YOU for changing my life! Love always!! Lucille."

I was happy for Aunt Lucille, of course, but I wished the flowers had been from Rocky instead.

Somehow, Mercedes talked Dad into going with her to the tennis courts on Saturday afternoon, and Mom and I were home alone. The phone rang about three-thirty, and Mom answered. When I heard her say, "We can't wait to see you, either!" I knew it was the Spenders.

But Mom certainly wasn't speaking for me. I *dreaded* seeing them. Especially Jerry, and most especially, Jerry's hand.

Mom hung up the phone and said excitedly that they were coming for dinner, and they wanted to bring a bucket of chicken, just like they used to in the old days. (Mom's supposed to make the salad.)

She went running off to the store and the house was quiet. I thought I was going to go crazy, my mind was in such a jumble. First of all, I was in a real quandary about Heather, and what I had come to think of as *"my terrible plan."* I couldn't forget Rocky sitting there on the tennis court and humming like a guru, explaining to Mercedes about the music of the spheres. Alone in the house, I shut my eyes and covered my ears and tried to listen for the humming of the universe, but all I heard was that same discordant sound that had persisted in my mind ever since my sweet Bribe lay dead and bloody on the freeway.

Thoughts of the Spenders pushed Heather out of my mind. A stupid little memory from long ago just wouldn't go away. I could see it all so plainly: The bucket of Kentucky Fried there in the center of the table, and all of us gathered around in happier times—little Jerry's legs swinging back and forth as he gobbled down his drumstick and licked his fingers, one by one. "Finger-lickin' good!" someone joked. "Jus' finger-lickin' good!"

I started watching out the window for the Spenders an hour before they were due. Mom had the huge salad ready, but for some reason she was still fussing around in the kitchen. Dad was reading the paper, and Mercedes was fooling around with her marbles and dominoes game, trying to figure out how to tell the winners from the losers.

"They're here," I breathed finally, as I saw a gray Mercedes sedan pull up in front of our house. All four doors burst open at once, and four people piled out of the car. I felt like running straight for the kitchen and right out the back door.

Nobody even mentioned Jerry's fingers, even though I knew it was on all our minds. He was a big kid for eleven, and looked exactly like Uncle Walter. My dad shook Jerry's hand without blinking an eye. Mom and Aunt Ginger hugged and hugged. My cousin Dawn came over to me and took me by both hands. "Hi, *again!*" she said gently, looking me squarely in the eye. Her own eyes were glistening with tears, and I liked her immediately.

"Come on, let's eat!" Uncle Walter said in a big booming voice when all the hugging was done. "The chicken's getting cold!"

Jerry sat across the table from me, and we studiously avoided each other's glance. It looked like the others were just going to let us work it out for ourselves.

Dad asked Jerry how the skiing was coming along. Jerry shrugged, looked quickly at his father, and smiled a sheepish smile.

"What skiing?" Uncle Walter asked sarcastically. "The rotten kid hasn't been on skis for years!" And then Uncle Walter reached over and bopped him on the head.

It turned out they never did go to that ski school in the Alps. Something had always come up to prevent them from going. One year Jerry had tonsillitis, another year, the flu. And one time, Uncle Walter said—the year he was made president of Allied Printing Company—("Congratulations!" we all shouted), they had to go to a printer's convention in Philadelphia.

After dinner everyone seemed to relax a little more, except for me. Jerry got a lot more talkative. He got into quite a long conversation with Mom, reminiscing about when he was little. He finally asked her what ever became of that old Etch-a-Sketch he got that Christmas. Mom had forgotten about it, I guess, but I remembered exactly where it was. "It's in the hall closet, Mom," I said quietly. "On that top shelf, remember?"

Mom jumped up and returned in a minute with the paper bag. Jerry pulled the Etch-a-Sketch out of the bag and unwrapped the newspaper, which he carelessly dropped on the floor. Aunt Ginger stooped to pick it up and was smoothing it out on her lap while listening to my father explain the differences between the two great leaders in the computer industry. I was watching Aunt Ginger out of the corner of my eye. She was nodding her head, pretending to be interested in what he was saying (I suspected), while at the same time idly scanning the old newspaper. Suddenly, without warning, she lifted the paper toward her and bent forward with an all-consuming interest. Then she lowered the paper and checked the date at the top. "My God!" she said. "My God!"

"What is it?" Dad asked, annoyed at the interruption.

"Listen to this," she whispered, "the dateline is Lucerne." Then she started reading in a quivering voice:

"A minibus carrying nine passengers from the Zurich airport to the Ski-Bird Ski School collided with a gasoline truck in a dense fog yesterday afternoon, killing all nine passengers and the driver. The truck driver, who emerged unscathed, was not cited. According to witnesses, the minibus crossed over the divider line while negotiating a hairpin turn and plowed into the side of the truck, which instantly burst into flames."

Aunt Ginger stopped reading. She wet her lips with her tongue and swallowed with some difficulty. "That's all it says," she said finally.

Uncle Walter reached over and took the newspaper from her lap. "Let me see that," he said, checking the date at the top of the page. Then he read the article to himself, silently mouthing the words. When he had finished, he put the paper down and looked at me. "Jesus Christ," he said. "That was the bus we would have been on. You saved our lives."

I stayed awake until I don't know what time, thinking about life, and people, and the way things happen, with every little thing depending on a million other things. For all those years I had been torturing myself about messing up Jerry's hand, and then it turns out I saved all their lives.

But did I, really? The more I thought about it, the more it made me wonder. What if the Spenders *had* gone on that trip? Is it possible that just their being there—the time it would have taken for them to get on that bus, loading up their luggage and so forth—maybe that time would have delayed the bus driver just enough for that truck to have come around the curve, and the accident would have been avoided. Did I save four lives, or cause the death of ten? Who could tell? Who could know for sure?

Suddenly and out of the blue, I thought of a name for Mercedes' game. Reaching for my flashlight, I got up out of bed and went into the kitchen and took a blank index card from the back of Mom's recipe file. I found a red marking pen in the drawer and wrote on the card in large letters, THE GAME OF LIFE. Then I went and propped up the card on the top of the board and made my way back to my room.

10

It was Sunday, two days before the Fourth of July, when Heather and Allan arrived in town. The Spenders had gone to visit friends in San Francisco ("Heather will be busy enough getting ready for her big day, without us getting in the way," Aunt Ginger had said), so just Mom and Dad and Mercedes and I were at home to greet them. Heather was even more flighty than usual. She had not even decided for sure what she was going to wear. She brought both her long flowered gown and a slinky light blue dress, but knowing Heather, she was just as likely to dress up as a firecracker for her wedding as anything else.

I was beginning to feel the pressure more and more. I couldn't act on my plan until the next day (which would be one day before the wedding), and one minute I felt sure I was going to do it, and the next minute I would be asking myself how could I even *think* of carrying out such a deceptive scheme. I really wished I could talk to someone about it, but that was impossible.

Heather had a crying jag around five in the afternoon, which surprised us all. She said Allan had been talking about something to do with Palm Springs, when all of sudden, he just got up and walked out of the room and then out of the house. We could see him striding past the window, shadowboxing with the wind.

Mercedes said, "Well, what's wrong with *him?*" and Heather started to cry. Mom brought her a cup of Ovaltine (that's what she used to drink when she lived at home), and when Heather saw it coming, in her old cup, she said, "Oh, Mom!" and just sobbed and sobbed. It was pretty awful.

It was obvious to me that Mom and Dad were going around in a kind of quiet desperation. It was like they had seen the mushroom cloud on the horizon, but were powerless to stop it.

Mercedes and Heather and I were all sleeping in my room that night, while Allan had Mercedes' room all to himself. Just before bedtime he said that while he was out walking he got a great idea for a song about two people falling in love at a recycling center (*"Their hearts were like a feather/As their cans were pressed together"*). We could hear him humming and strumming away deep into the night.

Long after Heather and Mercedes had dropped off to sleep, I was still awake, biting my inner lips until they were almost raw and forcing myself to lie quietly in the bed so as not to disturb Heather. When it came right down to it, could I really go through with my plan? I was convinced that the astrology column was nothing but a worthless hoax, but did I really have the right to manipulate one lie for another?

I was deep into these thoughts when Heather suddenly turned toward me and touched my shoulder. "Oh, Cairo," she said in a shaky whisper. "Are you awake? I just have to tell you something." She sat up in bed, leaning on one elbow, and rubbed her eyes. She looked like she was about seven years old.

"What, Heather?" I whispered. "What is it?"

She put her head in her hands and spoke so softly I could hardly hear her. "It really wasn't an accident, Cairo. He really did hit me with the stapler." Then her sobs almost drowned out her next statement. *"But Cairo, I can't argue with the stars! I have to marry him!"*

Well, that did it! I knew then that I was going to go ahead with my plan. I still didn't know if it was right or wrong, but I had to do it. Maybe I was rationalizing, but I told myself that the real responsibility for making choices ultimately rests with each individual. If Heather is stupid enough to believe in astrological predictions, the responsibility rests with her, and not in me for tinkering with them.

The next morning I left for work as usual, but this time with a mission. I grabbed a copy of the morning *Berkeley Bugle* from off the stack as soon as it came in and rang up the sale. Then I stashed it in the drawer with my purse and lunch.

There was a lull around ten-thirty, so that's when I got to work. First, I carefully clipped the entire "Stargazing with Gabe" column out of the paper. Then I got out the folder in which I had saved the column I had found before—the one with the forecast for Taurus that said, *"Cancel all plans for tomorrow. . . ."* And then, a little careful clipping and taping and it was done. I held my breath and made a copy. It came out like a dream.

I comforted myself with the thought that I hadn't added any new falsehoods to foul up the cosmos; with my clipping and copying, I had merely rearranged the astrologer's lies, and the music of the spheres was neither better nor worse. In other words, my conscience was clear.

The whole thing was so easy I couldn't believe it. When I got home from work I found Heather and Mercedes sitting at the dining room table, bleary-eyed from making red silk rosebuds, tied with pink ribbons. "They're favors for the wedding guests," Mercedes explained wearily, as Heather glumly tossed another little bouquet into a basket.

"Hmmm, very pretty," I said. And then I went into my act. "Heather, you know I really should tell you something. Even though it may sort of disrupt your plans, possibly . . ."

"What?" Heather demanded. "Tell me."

"Well, I happened to be reading your forecast for today in the very last copy of this morning's *Berkeley Bugle*, which I was saving for Mr. Gordon—see, he's a regular customer and he comes in every day for it. Anyway, I had to sell it to him, Heather, but first he let me make a copy of this." And I handed her my masterpiece. "I mean," I said, running my fingers along my eyebrow, "it looked very meaningful to me."

Heather practically grabbed the paper out of my hand. I think I heard Mercedes clearing her throat ever so softly, and when I looked over at her, she met my gaze with an intense stare and a slightly raised eyebrow.

The rest is history. Heather made a sound like "*Whoopee!*" and rushed off to find Allan. Mercedes and I were right behind her, and I noticed she plopped the forecast in front of him without even the slightest hint of tears. He cocked his head and read it, and then he read it again. He stood up and shoved his hands in the pockets of his coveralls and raised both shoulders in a long, slow shrug. I guess Allan must have been having second thoughts about the wedding too, because a few minutes later he was throwing his beat-up knapsack in his beat-up car and heading off down the street.

"He's probably going to Palm Springs," Heather said as we watched him go. "He's sitting Vernon Spook's house, and I'm supposed to be thrilled. It's in the middle of the desert, for God's sake, and *that's* where he wanted to spend our honeymoon!"

"Who's Vernon Spooks?" Mercedes asked.

"A famous rock star," Heather answered. "Haven't you heard of him?" And then she started laughing insanely. "God," she said, "you know, I think I just had a very close shave." She hugged us both together, one of us in each of her arms.

Mercedes rubbed the back of her hand alongside Heather's jaw. "I think you're right," she said, "a very close shave!"

I didn't say a word, because I was beginning to hear a new little glitch in the humming of the cosmos. The story I had told Heather about Mr. Gordon and the very last copy of the *Berkeley Bugle* was a pure and simple lie. I hoped it was no worse than lying to a burglar about a hidden emerald brooch, but I wasn't quite sure it was the same. I knew then that I would have to erase that lie someday and set things right again in the universe. Someday I'd have to confess to Heather exactly what I'd done. But she's certain to thank me and wonder how she could have been so completely taken in by the foolishness of astrology.

The Fourth of July dawned blue and mild, and Heather woke up singing. All the neighbors turned out early, and together we blocked off Cloverdale Circle with red, white, and blue crepe-paper streamers. We strung up the volleyball net on the Goldsmiths' lawn, as always, and Mr. Rogers rolled out their giant portable barbecue grill. Uncle Larry brought the potato chips, and Aunt Lucille even brought a guy she knew from work. I felt like a million, knowing I would soon see Rocky.

The Spenders arrived with a present for us—a gift certificate from Dreamer's Travel Agency, wrapped up in a red tube to look like a firecracker. "Please accept it," Aunt Ginger said, handing it to me. "We *had* to do something, and a little birdie told us you guys have never been to Disney World."

"Well, thanks very much," Dad answered at last (being the first to find his voice). "You know, this is very strange, because I almost entered a photo contest a while back, but . . ." He didn't finish his sentence.

The others let that pass, but I heard it loud and clear. Dad's eyes met mine, and he smiled and gave me a little fist salute.

Rocky and his mom arrived just as Heather put the hot dogs on the grill. I saw them huddling with Uncle Larry, all three deep in conversation, so I just waved at him and joined up with René and Jerry and Dawn and got a volleyball game going, while Mercedes and some of the other neighborhood kids were playing with the Game of Life, which she had set up on a card table on our front lawn.

Thank goodness Grandpa B was nowhere to be seen. I hoped he would just stay away.

He finally showed up about five in the afternoon, after we had eaten and while everybody was taking turns cranking the ice cream maker. I did my best to avoid him. Once, when I saw him heading straight for me, I ducked into the house and went to the bathroom. When I came out, he was talking to Rocky. Grandpa B had a cigarette in one hand and the other arm was slung loosely around Rocky's shoulder. Rocky's mom and Uncle Larry were still deeply involved in what looked like a very serious conversation. I went to take my turn on the ice cream maker, and pretty soon Rocky came over to join me.

"Your grandfather wants to take us some-where," he said.

"What? Where?"

"I don't know where, exactly, but—"

"Heck with that." I looked around and saw Grandpa B standing off by the porch, watching us. "Tell him no thanks for me, would you?"

"I want you to come," Rocky said simply.

"What's going on?" I asked. "Where does he want to go, and why should you want me to come? I don't get it."

Rocky took my hand. "Trust me," he said. "Okay?"

Something about the serious way he said it really affected me. I let him lead me under the crepe-paper streamers down the street to where Grandpa B's truck was parked. I turned around and saw the old man was following us. His head was lowered, and he was puffing on a cigarette as if his life depended on it.

When we got to the truck, Rocky opened the cab door and motioned for me to get in. I shook my head. I didn't even want to sit next to the dog murderer, so Rocky just jumped in ahead of me and sat between us.

No one spoke a word. Grandpa B drove alone in a very determined way, cussing under his breath (as usual) at all the stupid drivers on the road. We were heading out toward the Palm Acres section of town. Grandpa B owns several parcels of property around there. There are lots of warehouses and industrial-type buildings in the area, and the Humane Society's out that way, too.

Suddenly, I knew what he was up to. "I don't *want* another dog, Grandpa!" I said, my eyes flooding with tears.

He set his lips together and just kept on driving. I squirmed around in my seat and pulled a handkerchief out of my back pocket and blew my nose. Then I slumped down in the seat and said, "You might as well turn around and go back. I mean it. I'm not going to take it." And then I thought of something else. "Besides," I said, "they're probably closed today, anyway. It's a *holiday*, you know." The old fool had obviously not even thought about that.

Rocky turned to me and made a little frown. "Shhh," he said, and put his hand on mine.

Grandpa B made a sharp right turn and then began to slow down. I looked out the window and there was nothing there except a large expanse of empty field with a half dozen full-grown trees scattered around. And then I saw the sign. Grandpa B stopped the truck right in front of it. It wasn't a crummy homemade sign, but a real professional one, almost six feet high. It had a painting of a beautiful golden brown dog that looked just like Bribe on the top, and beneath it were the words

FUTURE HOME OF THE BRIBE MEMORIAL DOG PARK

in large black letters.

I looked at Grandpa B, and for one split second he looked back at me. Then he quickly averted his eyes, as his whole face began to twitch and his lips moved wordlessly. I knew that he was trying to tell me that he was sorry.

I don't remember much about the ride back home. Grandpa B and Rocky were talking about something to do with the National Rifle Association, but I was off in a world of my own. Grandpa B parked the truck down the block from Cloverdale Circle again, and the three of us walked back to join the others. I wanted to take my grandfather's arm, but I was just too shy, or too ashamed, or something (I don't know what) to do it. But I did walk close to him, and I managed to brush against his sleeve from time to time. At least that was a start. When we got back to the others, Heather came rushing up to us and said, "Hey, Grandpa B, you didn't get your hot dog yet!" and she led him over to the barbecue.

I could tell Rocky was anxious to get back to Uncle Larry. In fact, he told me just that. "I'm sorry I haven't been able to spend more time with you this afternoon," he said, "but Larry and I have been having *quite* a discussion."

"Oh, well," I said, "maybe later." What I really wanted to do was be by myself for a while. I went to my room and lay down on my bed. There was a single golden dog hair on my blanket, and I carefully picked it up and held it in a ray of sunshine. Who could measure the happiness and pleasure other dogs would experience because Bribe had lived and died? At least there was a purpose to *his* life, after all. Or, rather, could it be called a *meaning?* I thought again of Rocky's question to me that night when he was so upset: *What is the meaning and purpose of life, anyway?* Even though I had thought about the answer to that question myself many times in the past, now even the question didn't seem to make sense to me. What *is* purpose? What *is* meaning? It wasn't even clear to me what those words really meant.

I was exhausted, both physically and emotionally, but I had to know. I got up from my bed and took my thesaurus down from the shelf. I hadn't looked at it for months, not since a "Know Your Thesaurus" assignment Ms. Andes gave us last fall. I sat down at my desk and wrote out the simple question, *What is the meaning and purpose of life?* Immediately I spotted a problem. There were really two questions contained in that sentence: *What is the purpose of life?* and *What is the meaning of life?*

I looked up the word *purpose* first. I read every definition, and finally the word I was looking for seemed to hit me right in the eye; it was *work.* I rephrased Rocky's first question: *What is the work of life?*

Now I was getting somewhere. I tackled the word *meaning* next, and after a few minutes I had an answer. Some of the synonyms for the word *meaning* were "intention," "the end goal," and "reason for."

I went back to my bed and tried to put it all together. The universe is truth, Rocky had said, and I suddenly realized how that idea could be the key to it all. I went back to my desk and grabbed my pencil and scribbled down the following: *The purpose (or work) of life is to discover the meaning (or reason) for life. So what we have to do is learn all there is to know about ourselves and our universe. When we do that, when we know all truth, when we discover how it all began, what makes it run, and how it will end, when we discover all the truth in the universe, then we'll know the meaning—or the reason—for life. (If, indeed, there is one.)*

It all seemed so simple. I could hardly wait to tell Rocky. As I folded the paper and put it in my pocket, I caught a glimpse of myself in the mirror. I looked long and hard, and then I said out loud, imitating Mercedes' voice as best I could, "You're really nuts, you know that?"

My intention was to go find Rocky and hand him my little note, while announcing that I had thought it over and was now able to tell him the meaning and purpose of life. I thought he'd get a kick out of that. Only, he found me first. And he had something even more amazing to tell me. "I have some news," he said, "that you won't believe in a hundred years."

Uncle Larry and Mrs. Nevin walked up to join us. "Did you tell her yet?" Uncle Larry asked, his eyes all aglow.

Rocky shook his head. "Not yet. You tell her."

Uncle Larry put his hand on Rocky's shoulder and said, "Your young friend here and I are going to take a trip around the world!"

My knees almost buckled under me.

"We're a perfect match." Uncle Larry laughed. "I've got the money, and Rocky's got the enthusiasm and the guts."

Rocky joined in the laughter and stuck out his hand. The two of them shook hands vigorously, as Aunt Lucille and Mercedes and some of the others came to see what all the commotion was about.

"The first leg of the trip will be three months," Rocky started to explain to me.

Then Uncle Larry took over. "If all goes well—and I have no reason to doubt that it will—we'll extend it to a year. We're going to see whatever's out there. Right, Rocky?"

"A year?" I whispered. "A whole *year?*" I glanced up at Rocky. His face was shining with excitement. Once again I was overcome with simultaneous feelings of sorrow and joy.

The Spenders left early the next morning for Phoenix amid a raft of hugs and tears. The plan is for them to meet us at Disney World at the end of August, when Dad gets his vacation. We'll be gone for four days, and good old René says she'll take my place at the Copy Shop.

I had the day off, so Mercedes and I decided we'd try our luck at deprogramming Heather. Mercedes made a quick trip to the library on her bike, and when she returned we called Heather and the three of us sprawled out on the front-room rug completely surrounded by scientific books and journals.

Mercedes began the bombardment with known facts about the sun and moon and stars, the forces of gravity, and some elementary principles of wave mechanics.

"Now, Heather," she said, after twenty minutes of brilliant discourse, "will you please try to explain to me just *how*—that, is, by *what* force—could the pull of heavenly bodies at the moment of your birth *possibly* influence your personality—you know, like whether you are patient or hotheaded, or if you have a sense of humor or not, and even things like what day would be good for you to get out and socialize, or go buy a house or something—all that stupid stuff they tell you."

Heather made a face when Mercedes said, "All that stupid stuff they tell you," but then she thought a moment and answered, "We don't *know* yet what the force is, Mercedes. When you snap on an electric light, you can't see where the energy is coming from, can you? Well, it's something like that. Just because you can't see something doesn't mean it isn't there."

Mercedes nodded. "I see," she said solemnly. "But what about the 'gravitational pull' of the obstetrician, then, who's standing by the bed? Wouldn't that have some influence, too?" Mercedes flipped some pages in a magazine. "That fact is mentioned in an article here. See? It says the presence of the obstetrician has *six times* the gravitational pull of Mars, for instance."

"Good point!" I chimed in. "And what about the father, or the nurse? They're standing right by the bed, too! What about their gravitational pull?"

Heather cleared her throat. "Well, everybody has an obstetrician—or almost everybody," she said airily. "What difference could they make?"

Mercedes tried another question. "Okay then, what about jet planes?"

Heather laughed. "Jet planes? What about them?"

"They have gravitational pull," Mercedes said calmly. "Don't they? Do astrologers keep track of what jets were overhead at the moment of their client's birth? And speaking of that," she went on, "what sense does it make for astrologers to make their calculations at the moment of *birth*, anyway? The moment of *conception* would make more sense, wouldn't it? I mean, that's when a person's genetic characteristics are fixed, isn't it? Not at the moment of birth. Heck, by the time a baby's born, it's all put together already."

Heather shrugged. "I don't know. Maybe it's because no one knows the exact moment of conception."

"Aha!" Mercedes exclaimed triumphantly. "*You* said it, Heather. Astrologers can't play the game without a *time* to go by, can they? Especially since that's what they base their whole wobbly structure on."

"Another good point!" I said. "Now you're really rolling."

"Well, speaking of time," Heather said, "I want to call time-out. I need a cup of coffee."

When she returned, Mercedes tried another

tack. "Look here, Heather," she said, showing her an astrological chart with the familiar twelve signs of the Zodiac. "Have you ever heard of something called the 'precession of the equinoxes'? "

Heather laughed again. She was really in a pretty good mood. "Of course not, Einstein," she said.

"I'll simplify it for you then," Mercedes answered. "See, the Earth's axis . . ." She paused. "You know what the Earth's axis is, don't you?"

"Like, the ends?" Heather asked. "Like the North Pole and the South Pole?"

"Correct!" Mercedes said, while I applauded from the couch.

Heather stood up and took a fake bow. "I'm not a complete ninny, you know."

"Right!" Mercedes said, with just a hint of sarcasm. "Well, anyway, back to our axis—which is, actually, an imaginary line that passes through the poles—did you know that every twenty-six thousand years or so, as a result of the gradual westward movement of the equinoctial—"

"The what?" Heather asked.

"Okay. I'll simplify it for you more. What I'm trying to explain to you is that it's a scientific fact that the astrological sun signs are not lined up with their corresponding constellations anymore. For instance, a Virgo born two thousand years ago, when astrology was codified, would be a Leo today."

"So?"

"That's when Mercedes finally began to lose her temper. "What do you mean, 'So?' " she said loudly.

"Can't you see? Even if what astrologers say *did* have some basis in fact, they would be all wrong now! The constellations don't line up anymore! God, I can't believe how you—"

"Hey," I interrupted, sensing Mercedes needed to cool off. "Heather has her coffee. Let's you and I go get a soda or something."

Mercedes stood up. "Good idea," she said. "But don't go away, Heather. I've got a lot more to say!"

And she did. When we returned to the front room, Mercedes started talking about why astrology seems to be making a comeback in today's world. "It's people's need to believe," she explained. "People want simple answers, and that's what astrology does. It gives simple answers, and it talks about your favorite subject—*you.*"

Then she started reading parts of an article out of a publication called *The Skeptical Inquirer*, in which several studies were cited that showed how the predictions of astrologers failed miserably when exposed to scientific examination.

The talking (mostly by Mercedes) went on for several hours. I'd like to believe we'd made a change in Heather's thinking, but I don't know whether we did or not. At least we made a start in the right direction.

Since Allan went off with the car, Mom let me drive Heather back to Berkeley that evening. Mercedes came too, and we helped Heather move her stuff out of Frogpond and back to her old apartment. Her former roommates were delighted to see her again, and when one of them told her that Arthur had been trying to reach her, Heather seemed pleased and asked if he had left a number.

After we had carried the last of Heather's things up to her apartment and started for home, Mercedes noticed that Heather had forgotten her purse in the car. So I turned around and we went back, and I waited with the motor running while Mercedes ran back up to the apartment with it. When she returned, she was fit to be tied. "You'll never guess what Heather is reading now!" she said, slamming the car door so hard it made my ears pop.

"What?"

"One of her roommates—the one with the fake diamonds in her glasses—has lent her a book on *channeling*, and Heather thinks it's wonderful!"

Rocky invited me to go with him on Saturday while he had his passport photo taken. "And afterward," he said, "to celebrate, I want to take you out to lunch at DeMarco's." (The fanciest restaurant in town.)

Of course, I told him yes, but when I hung up I almost started to cry. I'm going to miss him so much. The worst part, I think—the part that makes me really miserable—is that I'm going to miss seeing a whole year of him that can never be brought back to life.

On our way to the photographer's, Rocky told me the very same thing! "You know," he said, "what hurts the most is that I'm going to miss seeing you during almost your whole seventeenth year."

"Gee, Rocky," I said softly, "I was thinking the same about you—that I'm going to miss a whole year of you that can never be brought back."

Just then we pulled up in front of Blaine's Professional Photography Studio, which sort of surprised me. "Does Blaine's do passport photos?" I asked. "I didn't think they would bother with little stuff like that."

"Really?" he asked, with a peculiar smile.

We went in and Rocky walked up to the desk. "I have an appointment," he said. "Rocky Nevin, for eleven o'clock."

I looked at my watch. It was only ten-thirty.

The woman at the desk checked her appointment book and smiled. "Oh, yes," she said. She pointed to a room in back of her, down a little hallway. "The costumes are in there, and the dressing rooms are in back. Take your time. Mr. Blaine is running a little late, as usual."

Rocky motioned to me. "Come on," he said.

He pulled me down the hallway and stopped at the glass door of one of the tiny rooms. "Look," he whispered, pointing through the glass.

There was a little alcove, all set up with Grecian urns and potted palms. Before I could say anything, he took me into the costume room and led me to the formal gowns. "Take your pick," he said, "but my favorite color is blue."

"What in the world . . ." I started to say, but

Rocky explained it all. "Somehow, I missed my Senior Ball," he said. A sly grin spread across his face. "I don't care about the dance, you know, it's that darned *photograph* of me at the dance that I need!"

"Rocky," I said, "are you making fun—"

He put his hand to my mouth, preventing me from saying anything further. "I thought I could make up for it by . . . well, I was hoping I'd get a chance to take you to yours, but now it looks like something else has come up, and that won't be possible. So this is the only solution, don't you see? I have to have that photograph to show to my kids some day, don't I? I wouldn't want them to think their old man was a real loser who couldn't even get a date for the Senior Ball, would I now?"

Later, over DeMarco's special chocolate mousse, I told Rocky the meaning and purpose of life. He stared at me a long, long time, and then he took my hand and whispered, "God, I'm going to miss you!"

"Me too, Rocky," I said, as he reached over and brushed a tear from my face.

And then for some reason he started to tell me about the love affair of a couple of Victorian poets he had been studying about in his English class. "It was called the romance of the century," he said. "You've heard of them—Elizabeth and Robert Browning. But do you know how their courtship started?"

I couldn't resist. "With a root beer?" I asked. "A large-sized root beer?"

He slowly leaned across the table and gave me a kiss, right in front of everybody. "No, you nut," he said, and I could tell he was having trouble keeping his voice steady. "It was with letters. The romance of the century, and it all started with letters . . ."